Californian Summer

Heartlines

Books by Pam Lyons

A Boy Called Simon
He Was Bad
It Could Never Be. . .
Latchkey Girl
Danny's Girl

Books by Anita Eires

Tug Of Love
Summer Awakening
Spanish Exchange
Star Dreamer
Californian Summer

Books by Mary Hooper

Love Emma XXX
Follow That Dream

Heartlines

Anita Eires

Californian Summer

A Pan Original

First published 1984 by Pan Books Ltd,
Cavaye Place, London SW10 9PG
9 8 7 6 5 4 3 2 1
© Anita Eires 1984
ISBN 0 330 28237 9
Phototypeset by Input Typesetting Ltd, London SW19 8DR
Printed and bound by
Richard Clay (The Chaucer Press) Ltd, Bungay, Suffolk

Chapter 1

Monday mornings really turn me on. I mean what girl wouldn't be over the moon at the idea of going back to school? Yes – you're right, I'm only kidding. But to be honest, I don't really mind school. I don't love it, of course, but it's a whole lot better than being dragged round the supermarket on a Saturday by a harassed, irate Mum who, because she works in a solicitor's office all week, tries to cram seven days' housework into one!

I guess the weather doesn't help, either. Take this last month. One would reckon that by the time it came to June in England we'd get just a little let-up from the deluge, wouldn't you? Last year – yes, I admit we did manage to get a few bright days for Wimbledon. But this year? Forget it! Every Sunday for the last six weeks it's rained. And when I say rained, I am understating again. It's poured! And what is there anyone can possibly do on a wet Sunday in Wimbledon – that is apart from watch re-runs of re-runs of pre-war films on the tele?

So I reckon, when it's all weighed up, you've got to agree that from my point of view, Mondays can sometimes offer a slight relief.

I don't want you to get me wrong. My weekends weren't always so bleak. Why, for three whole months they were really fantastic – but that's before I discovered Martin Wilde wasn't as wild about me as he'd had me believe. He was also, it worked out, pretty mildly enthusiastic about a certain sixth former called Diana Brown.

But give Martin his due, he did manage to brighten both our weekends for us for twelve whole weeks – undetected. And he was clever. Unbeknown to either Diana or me he would alternate which of the two non-school days he would take us out on. So, if one week Martin took me to the cinema on the Saturday – the following Saturday he'd take his tame red-head. Then he'd alternate the Sunday outings, too. 'Keep 'em guessing' – that must have been Martin's motto.

It came to a crunch when Mum and Dad took me to see the latest Bond epic one Saturday, when Martin had to babysit for his kid sister (great story that!) and who should be sitting bang in front of us but – you've guessed – lover-boy Martin and the delicious Diana? So, 'Hello Diana,' says I – followed shortly by a, 'Goodbye Martin!'

Weekends sort of lost their sparkle after that for a while. Don't misunderstand me, I wasn't in love with Martin – I mean how could I be, I was only fifteen? But he did have a nice racing bike and the added bonus of a generous allowance. As I said, he also brightened up my weekends in Wimbledon.

After Martin there was a long run of boyfriendless

weekends. Occasionally Claire, my best mate, would wander over and we'd play Scrabble or go for walks in Richmond Park. And once, we even decided to take ourselves down to Hampton Court where we managed, with no great difficulty, to get lost in the maze – and that's when I met Ramon.

Ramon was with a group of students, all discovering Britain in fourteen days flat! Ramon brightened up my life for the remaining four days he had left in London – but after that, things sort of settled back to their usual drab, and damp, routine.

Perhaps I should mention here that dear old Dad managed to bring some bright rays of sunshine into the household a few weeks ago. He'd read a book – given him by a no doubt well-meaning friend in the office – all about healthy living. You know the type of thing, the necessity of exercise in our lives. No more bought shop-cakes or quick-cook steak-and-kidney pies. All rubbish foods were taboo. It had to be whole to be healthy. 'From garden to gullet' was the general idea which, frankly, I found rather vulgar.

' "A family who plays together, stays together," ' Dad read out. 'Exercise – that's what we need. We spend too many weekends cooped up in front of the tele, or the video. I wish to heck I'd never bought that thing. It's killed conversation,' he expounded.

I kept on reading the daily newspaper but mumbled, 'What conversation?' thinking it would go unnoticed. A playful clip round my left ear meant Dad had heard all right.

'Anyway,' he went on, 'this book's convinced me we must change our habits — all of us, if we want to live to a healthy hundred!'

'Heaven forbid!' Mum groaned, raising her eyes to the ceiling.

'That's what I like, Sylvia,' Dad said, sounding smug. 'Someone who really tries. Well, I'm going to help myself to health.' (That *had* to have come from the book!) 'From now on, it's jogging in the mornings and wholewheat bread.'

That's when I'd opened my oversized mouth. 'Hey, I'll join you jogging, Dad,' I volunteered. I liked the idea — at the time.

That had cheered Dad up no end. 'Now that's the spirit, Carol!' he said, ruffling my hair like a dog's. 'We'll show Mum what we're made of. I'll get myself a tracksuit and you and me'll take a turn round Richmond Park. And I bet we're back before your mother is even out of her bed.'

So that's what we did. I wore my school tracksuit — not salubrious but serviceable — and Dad got all togged up in a bright orange one with a black trim. Then off we set at the incredible hour of seven-thirty. I have to admit that anything before nine on a Sunday didn't really exist for me before that. To be fair, it could have been the beginning of a whole new way of life. *Could* have been. But unfortunately we had only got half-way round the park before it began to pelt down and by the time we decided enough was enough, we looked like wet washing.

I think Mum could have been a little kinder. Still,

I suppose we did look a sight when we finally arrived home.

'Drowned rats!' she pronounced before disappearing to fetch some warm towels from the airing-cupboard. 'I don't know about getting healthy,' she said on her return. 'You're more likely to catch pneumonia.'

And that's what we did. Well, it didn't exactly turn into pneumonia as much as really streaming head colds.

Funnily enough, the health book disappeared back to Dad's office soon after that and, when the muesli ran out, the sugar-coated cornflakes made a great comeback. Which was a shame really because I got a taste for the stuff – even without adding milk. It was so nutty and crunchy.

I suppose some of my school mates would say I benefited from that little episode, but the truth was, having to spend three days at home with my Dad coughing, sneezing and generally dying all over the place wasn't my idea of a holiday. And I thought men were supposed to be the stronger sex. Some joke that is! I was just as ill as he was and yet in the end it was me running round looking after him, while he moaned and groaned in the big double bed getting through boxes of tissues and mountains of grapes!

I'll tell you, I was glad to get back to school.

Dad didn't go back to the drawing office – he's a draughtsman – until a week later. And even then he hummed and haa-ed about whether he was fit enough!

After that incident, Sundays sort of settled back into their usually dull routine and, as I said, when Mondays came round again I wasn't particularly perturbed.

Then this last Sunday an awful thought struck me. The summer holidays were going to be like a whole heap of boring Sundays! Six long, dragging weeks of them! It nearly blew my mind just thinking about it.

Last year had been bad enough but at least Mum hadn't been working full-time, and my Auntie Ann – Mum's younger sister – had lived round the corner. Not that I had a lot in common with her. It was my two cousins, Bobby and Joan, who I got on with. They were okay. We spent most of my fifteenth summer at the local baths and, like I said, the weather wasn't too bad so I managed to get quite a tan. Even so, by the end of August I was ready to go back to school.

But this year? This year was going to be unbearable! Auntie Ann and Uncle Dick had had to move up to Manchester. I say had to because there wasn't really any choice for them. Well, that's not strictly true. They could have stayed in Wimbledon but that would have meant Uncle Dick being made redundant. So he'd opted to keep his job and move with the company to Manchester. Naturally, the family went too.

And now the summer was almost around again and the outlook – forgetting about the weather – was decidedly bleak!

I mentioned my misgivings to my mother.

'Try and get a part-time job,' she suggested

brightly. Except that wasn't very bright of her. With over three-point-something-or-other unemployed, finding a part-time holiday job was like looking for a snowdrop in the desert, if you get my gist.

I did try, I have to tell you that. But then so did everyone else in my form . . . and the sixth form . . . and the upper sixth. And that was only our school! I believe two girls might have found work. A girl called Pattie Green is going to be taken on as a tea-girl. I think it's helped that her Dad's the director of the printing company which is to employ her. And a friend of mine, Becky Cohen, is getting to work in her aunt's boutique.

Otherwise nothing!

As I said, the summer's looking even more grey than a wet weekend in Wimbledon.

And then IT happened.

But I'll come to that in a minute.

Chapter 2

IT happened on one of those aforementioned Monday mornings.

IT came in a long airmail envelope with some pretty impressive postage stamps on — all the way from the US of A!

There was nothing unusual about this particular Monday morning – nothing special happened when Mum and Dad's alarm clock rang noisily in their bedroom next to mine. Nothing to even give a hint of what was to come just thirty minutes later while I was munching my way through my regular morning cereal and Dad was buried behind the daily newspaper. Mum, true to style, was trying to make the coffee, eat a piece of toast and open her mail at the same time. Suddenly she gave up and threw the letter across to me.

'Here, Carol. Make yourself useful,' she said, more than a little harassed. 'Open this letter – it's from your uncle by the looks of it. Read out what he has to say while I make your father some scrambled eggs.'

I sighed, and picked up the letter from where it had landed on top of the butter. A large greasy stain already half-obscured the address. Not deterred by the mess, I slipped my long finger nail (I should point out here that my nails are one – if not the only – good thing about me) under the sealed flap and extracted a couple of sheets of flimsy airmail paper – heavily scrawled with my Uncle Richard's elaborate handwriting.

'Well?' Mum enquired, glancing over her shoulder as she whisked eggs in a Pyrex basin, 'what does he have to say?'

I placed another spoonful of cornflakes into my mouth, then noticed that I'd added a milk stain to the greasy butter one on the letter.

'Well?'

Even Dad had put down his paper and was looking at me expectantly. I began to feel pressured.

'Hey,' I said, 'how comes I'm the one commandeered to read this? You know I can hardly decipher your brother's writing.' I waved the letter for Mum to take back – but she ignored me.

'What a fuss you're making,' she said. It's not often I ask you to do something for me, now is it?'

I tried hard to think of a million chores Mum usually got me doing but for the life of me I couldn't think of one. My mind had gone blank. Which was a good thing really because I hate having arguments and besides, if I were honest, Mum doesn't lay it on with me.

'*Dear Sylvia,*' I read out, '*I guess this is long overdue but quite a lot's happened recently. To cut it short – I've gotten married again.*'

'What?' My mother dropped the whisk she'd been holding. It clattered to the floor tiles, splattering raw egg down her camel-coloured skirt.

'The sly old dog!' Dad grinned across at Mum – but Mum certainly wasn't finding what I'd read out loud amusing! In fact she was looking far from happy, and it didn't help when she noticed the mess of her skirt.

'Shall I go on, or shall I stop and we'll have a discussion about Uncle Richard?' I asked sweetly.

Mum wet a towel under the hot tap and was rubbing furiously at her skirt. 'Go on for Heaven's sake, Carol,' she said impatiently. 'We might as well hear the rest of it. Married again – and him only divorced a year! I don't know what these Americans can be thinking of!'

I drew a deep breath and ploughed on. I was getting to like my new job.

'*Anyway, I should tell you that the new Mrs Walker is called Marcia and she's really something! Marcia lost her husband last year in a plane crash . . . anyway we met, fell in love and married so fast that there wasn't really time to let anyone know. I know you'll forgive me —*'

'Ha — that's just great!' Mum cut in, plonking plates of scrambled eggs in front of Dad and me. 'Just wait till my sister Ann hears!'

'Mum?' I handed the letter over to her. 'You finish it, will you?' I said. 'Then you can make your comments as you go along.' She took the letter then sat down and picked up her cup of coffee.

Mum sipped her coffee and started scanning the page. I could tell by her tight lips that none of it pleased her very much.

'Look here,' she said, scathingly. 'He's taken on a family, too. His new wife's got two boys. I ask you. . .?' She lifted the first sheet of paper and started reading the second. Pausing just long enough to gulp some more coffee.

'I wonder he can afford the extra responsibility. He says he's extending the house, whatever next? What with paying alimony to Stella . . . it's just fortunate they didn't have any children. . . .' She looked over at Dad. 'What are you grinning at?' she asked.

'Am I?' Dad's grin grew even wider.

'Yes you are!' Mum's cheeks were white — a sure sign she was angry. 'I don't see anything funny to grin at. Richard always was a hot head — getting into one scrape after another. He hasn't changed much if you ask me.'

'Oh, come on now, love, be fair,' Dad said, good-naturedly. 'He's made a good life for himself, by all accounts. The pay must be pretty good for pilots on one of the largest airlines in the world.'

'Money,' Mum snapped, 'isn't everything!'

I glanced at Dad, waiting for him to reply. It was rather like watching the tennis finals.

'It may not be everything, but it sure counts for something!' he volleyed.

Mum decided to ignore him and went back to the letter. I decided that as the most interesting news had already been imparted I might as well tuck into my eggs. And a second later, I wished I hadn't. The reason why I wished I'd not taken a forkful of eggs was because Mum screamed.

She screamed and then laughed and then joyously thumped my back. It was all too much for a Monday morning. My mouthful of eggs sprayed all over the tablecloth!

For a horrible moment I had thought I was going to choke to death right there at the table in front of Mum and Dad while they just ignored me.

It was like a slow-moving nightmare replay. Mum thrusting the letter at my father . . . Mum running round to point out something to him . . . and Dad shaking his head in surprise — and all the time me

15

trying to dislodge a piece of dry toast from the back of my throat while desperately gulping for air. Like a goldfish out of water.

Mum noticed my contorted face just in time. She rushed back to where I was sitting and started thumping me on my shoulders.

'Breathe through your nose!' she instructed, slightly panic-stricken. I shook my head trying to stop her hitting me. She was really hurting! Besides, I'd already managed to swallow the toast and suck in enough air to stop me choking.

I had just managed to wheeze and cough my way back to full consciousness when Mum noticed the eggs scattered over her clean cloth.

'For goodness' sake Carol!' she said, crossly. 'How can we possibly send you to California with your table manners?'

I started to make a really rude reply – like what the hell did I care about her silly cloth when I was choking to death in front of their noses? But I didn't say any of that because it dawned on me what she'd said.

IT had happened! My eyes, fairly large by normal standards, must have grown enormous.

Mum laughed at my expression.

'Well, do you fancy spending your summer holidays with your uncle in California?' she asked as if it were the type of question a girl gets asked every day. Like asking if I wanted sugar in my coffee or not!

'You've got to be joking!' I said, breathlessly.

'Would I joke about a thing like that?' Mum asked. That's when I knew she had to be serious. Mum never makes jokes about serious things.

I reached out and picked up the now very tatty and crumpled-looking letter which had come to rest in the marmalade dish.

I scanned over the first passages I'd already read and then got to the paragraph which had made Mum react so crazily.

'So, *as we won't be able to come over to you this year, we would like to invite Carol to spend part of the summer with us. It would be nice for her to meet Marcia's boys and, naturally, we'll pay all her expenses.* . . .'

I stopped reading and then went back, just to make sure I was really seeing what I thought I had seen. As I reread the words I was softly reading them out loud. I stopped and looked up. Mum's and Dad's faces were wreathed in smiles.

'Well?'

I stared at Mum. 'Well, what?' I said. My brain wasn't functioning any more. It was dancing round and round.

'Well, do you want to go, silly?' Mum asked.

'Are you kidding!' I exclaimed, jumping up and running round to hug first her and then Dad. 'Oh, it will be . . . be . . .' I searched for an adjective to describe how it would be. Then I shouted, 'Supersonicmarvellous!'

Mum burst out laughing. 'By that I suppose you mean yes?'

'Oh, yes! Yes, yes!' I twirled round the kitchen, hugging the letter to me.

'Hey, I thought a few moments ago you were against your young brother marrying again?' Dad said to Mum, a teasing note in his voice. 'Now you're about to allow your sixteen-year-old daughter to go over and share his house of iniquity.'

'What a load of nonsense you do talk sometimes, Ken,' Mum replied. 'Who am I to say what is right and wrong? After all, America's a different country and they have different customs, that's all.'

Dad pulled a face, then grinned across at me.

'Customs or not, young lady,' he said, 'I don't want you picking up any of their bad habits while you're over there, right?'

'What on earth do you mean by that?' I asked, flabbergasted.

'Never mind what I mean — just don't do it!' His words were ambiguous to say the least — but I knew what he was getting at.

I drew in a sharp breath. 'Honestly, Dad. . . .' I began, then stopped as I saw Mum making a sign for me to let it drop.

'Come on you two,' she said, suddenly gathering the dishes off the table. 'We're all going to be late this morning.'

I glanced at the kitchen clock. It had gone half-past eight.

'Oh, Heavens! I've missed the school bus,' I wailed. 'Will you give me a lift, Dad?'

'That will make me late,' Mum said.

'It's not so bad for you,' I called, running up to my room to get the books I needed for my morning lessons. 'If anyone says anything, I'll write you a note for tomorrow – okay?'

'Very funny!' Mum called back.

A few minutes later I'd pushed a pile of books into my tatty school bag, thrown on my raincoat and was back downstairs waiting by the front door.

'I'm ready!' I said, calling through to where Mum and Dad were busily putting away the clean dishes.

Mum came hurrying out to the hall to get her coat.

'You can't go out like that!' she said, staring at my feet.

I looked down, then burst out laughing. I was still wearing my slippers!

Chapter 3

At lunchtime, Claire and Becky and a couple of other fifth formers were all talking at once. Well, they weren't so much talking as firing questions at me! 'How are you getting there?' 'Do you need someone to carry your bags?' 'What will you wear?' 'How old are your uncle's step-children?'

In the end, I almost shouted at them to shut up! It was bedlam!

'Look, I've told you the lot already, all I know is that I've been invited, right? I don't know when, how, who and what. So do me a favour and let's change the subject.'

Becky pouted her bow-shaped lips — it's a habit which drives me mad. I can't stand girls who act like girls all the time when they don't get their way.

'Becky, please don't pout like that,' I said, nicely. 'I know you think you are a lot like Toyah but believe me it does horrible things to your eyes.'

'Cat!' Becky snapped.

I sighed and leaned back against the wall of the canteen where we had all had lunch. 'I am not a cat,' I said levelly. 'If I were, I'd tell you pouting made you look lovely, then laugh behind your back every time you did it, knowing you looked stupid.'

Becky leaned across the table and poked her tongue out at me. 'If you must know, I'm jealous,' she said. 'I want to go to California.'

We all laughed. That was the nice thing about our gang — we all got on so well we could be honest and say what we wanted.

'Don't be greedy,' Claire said. 'At least you've got a job for the summer which is more than any of us have to look forward to.'

Becky shrugged her narrow shoulders and hooked a lock of her incredibly long blonde hair behind her ear. 'I'd swap working in a boutique for my aunt for a chance to spend the summer with your uncle in America,' she said. Then smiled across the table at

20

me. 'Hey – how about it?' Do you think your uncle would like a Toyah look-alike round the place?'

'If anyone's going with Carol, it's me,' said Claire possessively clinging on to my arm. 'After all, we have been friends the longest.' She grinned up at me. 'Are you sure you don't need someone to help you with your luggage?' she asked.

'Oh, come on you lot. Let's drop the subject, shall we? I'm beginning to wish I'd never mentioned it the way you're all going on. And in any case, it was only an invitation –'

'*Only!*' Claire said. 'Boy, we should be so lucky!'

'You wouldn't have to ask me twice,' Pat, one of the other fifth formers said. 'Just think of it – hot, sunny days . . . the long golden beaches . . . barbecues . . . beach parties . . . boys!'

All the girls were following her every word and as Pat finished, Becky said, 'San Francisco . . . Los Angeles . . . boys!' She sighed deeply, staring at me out of narrowed eyes. 'You know something, Carol,' she said, coaxingly, 'working in a boutique's quite an experience. You really ought to try it – how about starting this summer?'

'Forget it!' I said, and laughed. 'It's my invitation and it's me who's going.' I stood up to leave and the other girls started to do the same.

As we wandered out of the dining-room, Claire and Becky fell into step either side of me.

'When do you think you'll go?' Claire asked.

I shrugged.

21

'Do you know what age your step-cousins are?' Becky looked decidedly interested.

'No, I don't, but I guess they must be fairly young because my uncle's younger than my mother so I expect his new wife will be younger than he is. Looking at it that way, her children must be younger than me, if you see what I mean.' I stopped. 'Are there such things as step-cousins?' I queried.

Claire and Becky hunched their shoulders.

'Who cares?' Becky said. 'If they're younger than you, does it matter?'

I stared at her and, catching my expression, she flounced away down the corridor.

'She's got a one-track mind,' Claire said. Then said, 'Boys!'

Claire and I began walking down to the doors which lead out to the playground.

'Still,' I said as we caught up with Becky, 'you've made me think.'

'Knew I'd be good for something one day,' Becky announced proudly.

I pushed her and she skipped away from us, down the steps.

'What are you thinking of, then?' Claire asked.

I stopped at the bottom of the stone steps and stared at my two friends. 'I was just thinking that maybe it isn't such a great idea – going to California. I mean if my two step-cousins, or whatever they are, are just little kids, I could find myself spending the summer as some kind of built-in babysitter!'

It was Becky who brought me back to reality.

'Listen, Carol – if you've got all that sun, sand and sightseeing going for free, what does it matter if you have to look after a couple of kids or a kindergarten full of kids? It's got to be fun!'

'You're right,' I said, brightly. I glanced up at the gathering grey clouds overhead and grinned. 'Anyway,' I added, 'it's got to be an improvement on Wimbledon – even on a sunny day.'

'Anything beats Wimbledon on a sunny day!' Claire said flatly.

'Aw, come on you two, let's go over and watch the football practice till the bell goes,' Becky called. 'All this talk about America's making me very unhappy. I need cheering up.'

'Come on, then,' I said, running ahead of Claire to where Becky was standing by the gate which leads round the back of the school to the games fields. 'Anything to keep Toyah happy.'

That afternoon I waited behind after our double lesson of geography. I knew it meant missing some of the break but it was important I talked to Mr Prentis.

'You wanted something?' my geography master asked, noticing me standing by his desk as he rubbed the day's notes off the blackboard.

'Yes, sir,' I said. Then added, rather self-consciously, 'I wondered if you could recommend a book I could read on America – California actually?'

Mr Prentis lifted his shaggy eyebrows in surprise.

'Any particular reason?' he asked. 'I don't usually get requests for extra reading material.'

I watched him replace the blackboard duster, then slap the chalk off his hands on to his already dusty trousers.

'Well, you see, sir, I've been invited to spend the summer with my uncle in America,' I explained.

The eyebrows lifted sufficiently for me to see the blue eyes light up with interest, which in turn encouraged me to tell him about the possibility of my spending at least four weeks in California.

'California, eh? Very interesting,' he said, giving me his full attention. 'Any particular place?'

'Yes, Los Gatos,' I replied, remembering where my uncle lived.

'Now let me see . . . that's between San Francisco and Los Angeles, if my memory serves me right,' Mr Prentis said, stroking his chin thoughtfully.

'Is it?' I asked, impressed by his immediate recall.

He smiled, then nodded. 'It's a very beautiful area – surrounded by some of the most incredible natural phenomena in the world. You're a very fortunate girl, Carol.'

'Yes, sir, I know,' I said. Then added, 'That's why I'd like to do some reading up on the area before I actually go.'

'Very wise,' Mr Prentis remarked, but it wasn't said in a patronizing way, just sort of . . . well, friendly. 'And you want me to recommend some reading?'

'If you wouldn't mind?'

'Mind, my girl?' He laughed. 'It will be my pleasure. I've got some literature at home. I'll sort it out and let you borrow it.'

'Oh, I didn't want to put you to any trouble,' I said, quickly. 'I was quite prepared to buy some books.'

He led me to the classroom door. 'Why waste your money?' he said, helpfully. 'I'll be glad that my books will come in useful.' He glanced at his watch. I could tell he was worried in case he missed tea in the staff room.

I thanked him and was about to walk away when he called me back.

'Why not think about making your holiday to California into a project?' he suggested. He gave me a rare smile. 'Or is that pushing your sudden awakening to the pleasure of geography too far?'

I lowered my head. His jibe had hit home. Geography had never been one of my best subjects.

'I think I'd like to do that, Mr Prentis, sir,' I said, after a minute. 'It could give me something to remind me of it when it's over.'

He grinned again, lighting up the amazing clear blue eyes under the grey overhang of his bushy brows. 'You never know,' he said, 'you may even enjoy doing it once you get started, eh?'

I smiled up at him. 'Oh, I will, sir!' I said. But he wasn't taken in by my burst of enthusiasm.

'Well, let's wait and see, shall we?' he said. 'Let's wait and see.'

Chapter 4

'That's settled then!' My mother heaved a sigh of relief and placed the red, white and blue cardboard wallet, holding my air tickets, safely in the side of her handbag. She fastened the clasp and, looking up, smiled at the girl behind the travel agency counter.

'You'll find details of flight times, booking-in times and general tips in the folder,' the girl said, returning Mum's smile. 'But don't forget, if there's anything else you need to know we're here to help.' She turned to me. 'I hope you have a fabulous holiday in America,' she said. Then added, 'I did, I can tell you. It's unique.'

I had the urge to stay and ask her a million and one questions but my mother had already turned and walked to the door. So I just thanked the girl and left. I didn't need Mum to tell me we had a tight schedule. She had already pointed out where she wanted us to go to buy some new clothes for me.

Her first stop was Marks and Spencers. Her idea – not mine. Not that I don't like their things, it's just that I'd rather search around the boutiques for my clothes. Places like the jean shops. But as Mum was footing the bill, I tagged along. I had the feeling it wasn't going to be a very happy experience – Mum was already glancing at her slim gold wristwatch.

'Come on Carol!' she called, hurrying along the crowded street. 'At this rate we'll never get everything you need!'

'Well, let's leave the shopping – I'll come up to town on Thursday when it's late-night opening to get what I need,' I suggested.

'Out of the question! Last time you did your own shopping you spent a fortune on rags which lasted through one wash.'

'That's not true!' I exclaimed, glaring furiously down at a small child who had stamped on my toe.

'I'm not arguing,' my mother told me, hurrying even more through the swell of the Saturday morning shoppers.

'Mum!' I called, leaning forward and grabbing her arm. She stopped so abruptly that I bumped into her.

'Watch where you're going, Carol – that was my foot you trod on.' Mum bent down to massage her toes and nearly got toppled over by a group of punks who pushed past. I caught her elbow and steadied her.

'Let's cut down these steps into Great Marlborough Street and go round the back way to Marks,' I suggested.

Mum nodded and pushed me ahead of her. I turned to my right and ran down the narrow stone steps, waiting when I reached the bottom for Mum to catch up.

'That's better,' my mother said, slowing her pace a bit as we walked along the comparatively empty road which ran parallel to Oxford Street. 'Now, let's just go over what you'll need.' She took a list from her jacket pocket and a pencil and, with her bag securely over her arm, she began to itemize the clothes she'd decided I'd need.

'Underwear, a new nightie – I suggest cotton, it's cooler than a man-made fabric.'

'Okay,' I said. I really wasn't interested in what I wore in bed. It was the daytime clothes I cared about.

' . . . a new toilet bag –'

'My old one's all right.'

'Don't interrupt. Toilet bag, shorts, jeans and tee-shirts –'

'Do we have to buy those in here?' I asked as Mum pushed open the heavy swing doors which led to the store.

Mum looked up and scowled. 'We're not going to have another row, now are we, Carol?'

I feigned surprise. 'Of course not,' I said. 'I was only asking –'

Mum went ahead of me and began climbing the stairs to the ground floor. 'Well, please don't,' she said. And I knew from the look on her face that it would be pointless arguing. Mum was just as likely to turn round and go all the way back home leaving me with nothing.

I ran up the steps behind her, deciding to give in gracefully. After all, I thought, I might just be able to buy some things which I liked with the money out of my post office savings account when I got over to America.

Five minutes later, Mum was standing in front of the swimwear section, looking at bikinis.

'Aren't these super?' she said, holding up a bright blue-and-white one.

'You know me, I don't like blue,' I said ungraciously.

My mother shot me a look. 'It's not for you,' she said. 'It's for me.'

'Why do you need a bikini?' I asked, surprised.

'To take to Mallorca,' she answered, then picked up a similar costume but in a bright pinky colour.

'Mallorca?' An assistant who was passing turned and smiled – she was so tanned I reckoned she must have just returned from the island. 'Since when are you going to Mallorca?' I asked.

'Since you are off to California, miss,' Mum said, smiling broadly at my open mouth. 'Don't look at me like that,' she said. 'It was your Dad's suggestion – we thought we'd treat ourselves this year.'

For some reason I felt really let down. Sort of . . . well, cheated. Shut out.

'So with me out of the way, you two are going on holiday on your own? Very nice!'

Mum replaced the pink bikini and held on to the

blue-and-white one she'd first chosen. 'You sound as if you resent your father and me having a holiday.' Mum said, meeting my glance.

'No, it's not that,' I said, backing down, 'it's just that if I'd known –'

'You'd have rather come to Mallorca? Well, pet, we can always write and tell your uncle you've changed your mind.'

'Never!' I said, quickly – and Mum grinned.

'See. Now come on, let's buy the basics here and then I'll let you drag me round those dark, airless boutiques to see what you want.'

'Mum, you're lovely,' I said, giving her a bear hug.

'Go on with you.' She pushed me off playfully. 'You're only saying that,' she said, 'because you want my money!'

It was half-past four by the time we'd bought everything. Well, nearly everything. I still hadn't seen any tee-shirts I'd liked and I couldn't get a pair of sandals, either.

'You can get those by yourself on Thursday,' Mum conceded after we'd tramped in and out of a hundred shops! 'Right now I need a hot cup of coffee and a sit down. Come on, let's go over to Peter Robinson's – there's a nice restaurant on the first floor – an off-shoot of that health food restaurant, you know – Cranks. We can get a coffee and a nice gooey cake. It will set us up before we attempt the journey home.'

I didn't need any coaxing, my feet were as tired as Mum's and I was beginning to get a headache.

*

When we were finally seated at a pine table, on high stools, surrounded by hanging pot plants and other harassed shoppers, Mum said, 'Do you realize it's only another two weeks before you go?'

I nodded, my mouth full of spicy carrot cake.

'Nervous?' she asked.

Again I nodded.

'You're not really, are you?' she enquired, a look of worry creasing her smooth forehead.

I finished the cake in my mouth and sat back. 'I am, and I'm not,' I said. 'I'm not really worried about flying to America on my own – it's the arriving which scares me stiff. I mean, what happens if I hate it? Or I don't like Uncle Richard's new wife and her two kids? I can hardly say "thanks a lot" and turn round and come home, can I?'

'Well, you could . . .' Mum began, then added, 'but they may think it's just a tiny bit rude. After all they are paying for your flight.'

'That's exactly it,' I said, plaintively. 'They're paying. It will make me feel obliged to them – all the time.'

'But that's a silly way of looking at it, pet,' Mum said. 'After all, you should consider it a gift. And you don't have to feel under any sort of obligation when you're given a gift, now do you?'

'Putting it that way . . . well, no,' I said. 'Still, I wish you'd told me before that you and Dad were planning on going to Spain.'

'We didn't know ourselves until last night. We saw one of those cheapies in the evening paper. Not for a moment did we think we'd actually be able to book one – but we did. Do you realize it will be the first holiday your Dad and I will have had on our own since – well, our honeymoon?'

I fingered the rim of my cup. When I looked up, Mum was watching me. 'I guess we all have to get used to changes,' she said, wistfully. 'We've been such a close unit over the years it's going to come hard learning to live separate lives again.'

'Why should we have to?' I asked, puzzled.

Mum leaned over and touched my hand, squeezing it gently. 'You're growing up, Carol,' she said. 'One day soon, not very far away, you're going to want to make your own life – it's only natural – and your Dad and I have got to get used to the idea. This holiday with just the two of us will be a good opportunity of getting to know each other again as individuals – not being just a Mum and Dad.'

Her words worried me. Not about them getting used to being individuals again – but the bit about me growing up . . . making a life of my own. To be honest, the prospect of ever leaving home had never crossed my mind. And now that it had been brought up, I didn't know if I liked the idea.

I finished my coffee and glanced about me. The table opposite was occupied by three girls – not much older than Claire, Becky and me but they all looked sort of sophisticated, working girls – perhaps even living away from home. The idea unnerved me, and for the first time since my uncle's letter had arrived, I wondered if I was doing the right thing. Did I really want to go? The holiday had suddenly taken on a completely new look. It wasn't so much a holiday as the first step to growing up. And at that precise moment, I wasn't too sure I wanted to take that step — not, yet. Not for a while, at least.

Chapter 5

'Please fasten your seat belts, extinguish all cigarettes, and make sure your seats are in an upright position. Thank you,' the chief stewardess announced over the plane's tannoy.

I glanced down to make sure my belt was securely fastened and realized that somehow I had got mine tangled up with the one belonging to the woman who was sitting next to me. The result was that she was having great difficulties in making hers meet across her middle.

'Oh, I'm sorry,' I said, unlocking the catch to mine and disentangling hers.

She laughed. 'Boy, I was worried there for a moment,' she said with a strong American accent, 'I thought I must have put on at least ten pounds!'

She took the now released belt and easily fastened the clasp.

'Phew! That's a whole lot better,' she exclaimed. She settled back in her seat as the plane gathered speed along the runway, then smiled across at me. 'This your first time?'

I shook my head. 'I've flown before,' I said, 'but not to America, if that's what you mean. I flew to Benidorm once, and once to Paris on a school trip.'

The American woman smiled again, showing perfect, pearly teeth. 'Well, we're going to be travelling companions for at least eight hours, so I guess we should introduce ourselves. I'm Mary Jo Mailer and this here,' she said, leaning back against the seat as a younger version of herself leaned forward and smiled at me, 'this is my youngest, and her name's Louisa. But we all call her Lou, don't we hon?'

'Sure do, Mom,' Louisa said.

'I'm Carol,' I told my travelling companions, then added, 'my folks usually call me many things but I guess I shouldn't repeat them here.' It was meant as a joke but, by the blank expressions on Mary Jo's and Lou's faces, I obviously hadn't gauged their humour. I shrank back against my window seat and stared out at the pitchy, black night. It was odd because although it was after midnight, I didn't feel at all sleepy. In fact, I was wide awake.

With a gentle sensation the Jumbo lifted off the ground and began its assent. The noise of the engines throbbed through the body of the plane.

'Cabin crew may release now,' the captain's voice said over the system. A ping! sounded and I noticed that the little sign over each bank of seats which said *You may smoke now* had lit up, but not the one about unfastening the seat belts.

Mary Jo noticed what I was looking at.

'They usually like you to keep your belt fastened until they have made their assent and are cruising at the required altitude,' she told me, knowledgeably.

'Oh?' I couldn't help thinking she had a nice face but I had the feeling that she was older than she looked. A strict follower of the Jane Fonda workout regime, I concluded.

The cabin lights were dim, but here and there people had switched on their overhead reading lamps. I looked up and tried to decide which was mine. The panel above our heads looked like a mini computer – but then with a plane as big as the Jumbo, I guessed it was natural.

'You want your reading light?' Mary Jo asked, and when I nodded, she reached up and deftly located the one for my seat.

'You seem to know all about aircraft,' I said, politely.

The nice, open face creased into a smile. 'I ought to,' she said. 'I used to be an air hostess.'

'You did? How exciting!' I exclaimed.

'It's not as glamorous as you'd believe,' she told me, 'but heck! we had some fun times.'

'Like meeting Pop!' Lou said, raising her eyebrows. I reckoned she was about a year younger than me – maybe two. She still wore braces on her teeth and her silky blonde hair was held off her face in a fat plait which fell half-way down her back.

Mary Jo laughed. 'That sure was fun!' she said.

'Is he American too?' I enquired.

'Mom's not American!' her daughter exclaimed. 'She's from London, aren't you, Mom?'

I stared open-mouthed, hardly believing my ears.

'Yeah, I was from good old London,' Mary Jo continued, 'but that was over twenty years ago now so I guess, as years go, I'm more true blue American than British.'

Curiosity got the better of me. 'Was it one of those in-flight romances? Air stewardess and a passenger?' I asked.

'I wish it had been,' the woman said. Then added, 'If it had been I might see more of Monte. No, I'm afraid I got landed with the pilot – if that's the right phrase to use in the circumstances.'

'Big romance, eh?' Lou said, sighing dramatically and pulling a face.

'But it is.' For a moment I dreamed of how lovely it would be to fall in love with someone as dashing and impressive as an airline pilot. 'My uncle's a pilot,' I said. 'He works for United. That's where I'm going now – to stay with him.'

Mary Jo looked up from scanning the in-flight magazine she'd extracted from the pocket of the seat in front. 'That's interesting. United is the company I used to work for – Monte's still flying for them. What's your uncle's name?'

'Walker,' I told her.

Mary Jo sat up straight in her seat, her face alight with surprise. 'Not Richard Walker?' she asked.

I nodded wondering what all the excitement was about.

36

Lou popped her head forward and stared at me, then looked at her mother. 'Is that Uncle Richard?' she asked, puzzled.

'Sure is, popsicle,' she said. She shook her head as if to make sure she was hearing right.

'Do you know him?' I asked.

Mary Jo looked as if she was going to hug me and I shrank back a bit. I never was one for physical demonstrations.

'Know him? Heck, I almost married him!' she said, smiling at me and still shaking her head from side to side so that her hoop earrings swung like pendulums against her cheeks. 'Well, isn't this just incredible?' She settled back in her seat and stared up at the roof of the plane. I could tell she was going over old memories. At last she turned back at me. 'You know, honey, that man, he has such charm! He had all of us stewardesses swooning over him. What a dish!' She stopped enthusing for a second as a frown puckered her smooth forehead. 'Didn't I hear he got divorced from Stella, though?'

'He's married again,' I told her, to keep her in the picture. 'My new aunt's called Marcia.'

Mary Jo clapped her hands gleefully. 'Marcia? I wonder if it's the same Marcia who flew with us?'

I shrugged. How should I know? 'She's a widow – well, was,' I said, remembering my uncle's letter. 'And she's got two young sons.'

'It's got to be the same Marcia,' Mary Jo decided. 'Boy, they sure didn't waste any time!'

'Yes?' I wasn't sure if I was supposed to make a

comment or not. She seemed to be talking more to herself than to me.

'But you're wrong,' she said, and before I could ask what about, she told me, 'her boys aren't that young – not if it's the Marcia I think it is.'

'Oh?'

Mary Jo shook her head, then grinned. 'Her eldest – Chuck – has got to be at least eighteen, he'd be a freshman now. And that would make Paul Junior, let's see, yes, fourteen.'

'Really?' Suddenly my whole image of the forth-coming holidays was shattered. Eighteen and four-teen? Heck! I'd hardly be babysitting, would I?

The stewardess appeared by our row of seats and, leaning low, asked if any of us would like a pillow and a blanket.

'Make it three, honey,' Mary Jo said, taking charge. 'We should try and get some sleep, or we'll all turn out looking like zombies at San Fran.'

The stewardess smiled and walked away. She returned a few seconds later and handed out our bedding.

'We'll be coming round later with light refresh-ments for those who would like some,' the hostess informed us. Then added, 'Have a good sleep.'

I arranged myself as comfortably as I could in my semi-upright position.

'Here, lower your back-rest,' Mary Jo said, pressing a button in the arm of my seat. The seat slipped back so that I was half-lying along it.

I suddenly felt tired. I guess it was a combination of

the pent-up excitement, nervousness, and the gentle humming of the engines.

I was about to drop off to sleep, when I heard Mary Jo say, 'We'll be almost neighbours, while you're over there — unless Richard has moved off his Redwood mountain.'

'He's still there,' I said, sleepily, wishing she'd go to sleep.

'Well, we're just down in San José,' she droned on. 'We'll have to get together — let you kids have a pool party . . . it will be just great!'

I didn't answer her. I was just too tired. Somewhere behind me I heard a baby crying . . . and crying. . . .

And when I started to dream I still heard the wailing — only it was coming from two tall, suntanned boys. They were following me round in massive nappies, with dummies sticking out of their mouths. Somehow in my subconscious I knew they were Chuck and Paul Junior and I couldn't understand what I was expected to do. If they'd been babies, it would have been easy. But two huge grown-up boys posed other problems. They were still following me as I began to wake up — only they weren't crying any more, they were cooing.

I sat up with a start. Mary Jo and her daughter were still sleeping. As carefully as I could I straightened up and rubbed the back of my neck which was stiff. Behind me I heard the baby making gurgling noises and I assumed it was being fed.

I smiled to myself as I remembered my dream and made a mental note not to burst out laughing when

I met Chuck and Paul. But just the memory of the oversized nappies and dummies would be enough to start me off.

I rubbed my eyes and yawned then peered out through the small window. I expected to see some sort of light on the horizon but it was still dark. And then I remembered Mr Prentis had explained that, as I'd be flying West, I'd be flying into the night-time. It was a weird sensation.

'Would you like some refreshment?' a voice whispered.

I turned round to find the stewardess smiling down at me, silhouetted in the dimmed cabin lights.

'I'd love a drink of something,' I said.

'Orange juice?'

'That would be lovely,' I said, softly.

I straightened the blanket and put my seat back into the upright position, just as the stewardess returned with a small tray. She handed it to me. On it was a small can of juice, a glass with ice in it, and a packet of biscuits. I smiled my thanks.

She leaned over and switched on my reading light. For a moment I thought the movement would disturb my two sleeping companions, but they slumbered on, their blankets rising and falling evenly. I sighed a sigh of relief. I didn't fancy having to participate in another long dialogue. I was still too tired. And besides, I wanted time to think. After all, if Mary Jo were right about Marcia's family, I had a lot to think about. I'd never shared a home with two boys before!

Chapter 6

Crispy bacon, scrambled eggs and waffles were served for breakfast. The fabulous aroma of it filtered through from the galley. When it came on little plastic trays, I thought it was a feast. And by the look of everyone else's empty trays ten minutes later, I hadn't been the only one hungry.

As the plane journeyed on, the first watery fingers of the long-awaited dawn crept on to the horizon. I watched fascinated and then, without realizing it, I must have slipped off to sleep again.

Mary Jo tapping my arm woke me. 'We're just circling for our final descent,' she informed me. 'Better fasten your seat belt.'

I thanked her, then turned to look out of the window. Bright golden sunlight shone through. The amazingly blue skies were dotted here and there with powder-puff clouds, and far below I could see the wide expanse of the Pacific Ocean, and the jigsaw outlines of what I assumed was San Francisco bay.

'Looks great, doesn't it?' Mary Jo craned her neck to see. I caught a drift of flowery perfume and realized that she'd obviously taken the time, while I'd been asleep, to freshen up.

The thought that I must look a mess shot through my mind.

I gazed up at the panel above my head, but its instructions were clear — all seat belts had to be fastened, ready for landing. Well, there was nothing else for it but to try to comb my hair and freshen up with the aid of my handbag mirror.

I fumbled in my cluttered bag until I found my mirror and then extracted my lip gloss.

The face which stared at me was all eyes and pale cheeks. My mascara had smudged under my eyes and there wasn't a trace of lip gloss. What's more, my usually glossy brown hair looked dull and lifeless.

Great! I thought miserably. What a fantastic vision you're going to present for the first time! I frantically added some fresh shadow to highlight my light blue eyes, then ran a damp tissue under my lashes to dislodge the caked mascara. Just as I was running the lip gloss to my lower lip the whole thing fell apart in my hands.

'Oh, drat!' I exclaimed, beginning to feel panicky and terribly nervous.

'Hey, don't get in a tizz,' Mary Jo said, handing me a tissue and picking up the plastic case from where it had fallen on her lap. 'You're just going to love everything about California, you'll see.'

I managed a watery smile. 'I'm just a bit worried my uncle won't recognize me,' I said. 'He hasn't seen me since I was ten.'

Mary Jo laughed loudly. 'He'll recognize you all right. Except that he's male and you're female, you couldn't be more alike. The same smooth brown hair and high cheekbones. The same light blue eyes. And from what I've heard from you, I reckon you've the same sense of humour.'

'Well, I hope so,' I said. I pushed everything back

into the jungle inside my handbag. 'Because from the way I look, he's got to see the joke.'

'You look very pretty,' Mary Jo assured me. 'Believe me – you'll knock 'em cold!'

I smiled politely, but I wasn't convinced. I glanced across at Lou. She sat there cool and almost sophisticated. And here was I at least two years older, shaking like a kid on her first day at school. I drew in three deep breaths – just as Mum had told me to do since I was a kid. It was supposed to calm you down, steady your nerves.

I took another three and waited for the calming effect to take hold. It didn't come – and all it did was to make me feel more sick!

I stared down at the fast-approaching runway and wondered if it was too late to get off and go back home. At that moment I would have given anything to be lying on a beach with Mum and Dad in Mallorca. Anything!

Chapter 7

Oakland Airport was totally unexpected. All open plan with sliding glass doors and picture windows. One moment I was claiming my luggage – and then the next, I was riding up an escalator into yet another glass-sided open-plan area.

Uncle Richard was standing at the top of the moving stairway. He stood out a mile. Tall, handsome and wearing the biggest grin you've ever seen.

'Carol?' he cried, disbelief and excitement colouring his voice. 'It can't be? My God, but you've grown!'

I reached the top of the moving staircase and found myself swept off my feet up into his arms. He swung me round and then unceremoniously dumped me back on the ground.

Still with his arm round my waist he said, 'Look at me and my bad manners. I want you to meet Marcia. Carol, this is my wife.'

I looked across at a smiling-faced woman who had to be as old as Mum. She wasn't a bit as I'd expected her to be. All sort of willowy and blonde – a sort of slimmed-down Dolly Parton. Oh no! Marcia was short and a little plumpish. She wore a pair of baggy jeans and a blue checked shirt with a bright scarlet neckerchief tied at her throat. Her cowgirl outfit was completed by a pair of bright red studded ankle boots.

'I've got to tell you something, Carol,' she said, holding out her arms and placing a hand on either side of my shoulders, 'you've grown somewhat since your uncle last saw you, right?' She grinned up at my uncle and shook her head. 'He had me believe you were no higher than a hedgehog and at least five years younger than you are. You wait till Chuck and

Paul Junior catch a glimpse of you – are they in for a shock! They all but had you in diapers.'

'You're joking!' I looked up at my uncle. 'Really!' I said. 'And from what you wrote to Mum in your letter, I thought Chuck and Paul were running around in a playpen.'

We all started laughing and then Mary Jo appeared on the scene, with Lou in tow looking tired and grumpy.

'It is Marcia, isn't it?' she exclaimed and then the two women were hugging each other and my uncle was kissing Mary Jo's perfectly made-up cheek and they were all saying how great it was to see each other again. And how they must all meet up.

'I'm throwing a lawn party next Friday,' Mary Jo said, extracting herself from Marcia's embrace. 'Now you all most come. It's my eldest daughter's eight-eenth birthday so it'll be great for the kids. If you like they can all stay over and spend the day round the pool with my Danielle and Lou. We've lots of room.'

'That sounds great,' Marcia said, glancing up at her husband. 'Can I ring to confirm? I'm not too sure what our plans are at present. I'm afraid it's all a bit in the air. Let me call you.'

'You do that!' Mary Jo said happily. She took hold of Louisa's hand. 'Come on, popsicle,' she said, 'we'd better go and find your Daddy.'

We watched her and Lou disappear along the passage and then Uncle Richard picked up my case and Marcia took my holdall from me and with one on either side, they walked me out of the airport to the car park.

Marcia grinned and two dimples appeared in her suntanned cheeks. 'I love Mary Jo, but oh, boy! does she talk! I bet you had a non-stop conversation all the way across, didn't you, Carol?'

'Sort of,' I admitted. I hurried to keep up with them both as they dodged in and out of the parked cars. Eventually we came to a halt by the side of a sleek, silvery station wagon which looked rather like a boat!

'Don't worry yourself about the size of this old Dodge,' my uncle said, catching my expression, 'we only use it on rare occasions — like when we take the whole family — plus dogs — out.'

'Dogs?' I asked.

'You bet!' Marcia said, passing my holdall over to Uncle Richard who was arranging my case in the back of the car. 'I don't think a home's a home without a dog or two round the place.'

My uncle slammed shut the hatch-back and threw the keys across the roof to his wife. 'You drive, sweetheart,' he said. 'I'll sit back with my niece and point out all the local highspots to her.'

'Hey, that's not fair,' Marcia said. 'I drove down here.'

My uncle grinned, but gave in. 'Throw them back then,' he said. 'And don't talk to me about the Women's Lib movement, okay?'

We all clambered into the car, which I swear was built for an army! and then my uncle switched on the ignition. Purring like a large cat, the 'ship' cruised out of the parking area and joined the stream of traffic on the motorway.

'We usually use my Honda for nipping about in,' Marcia told me, leaning over the front seat to talk to me, her chin resting on her hands. 'A lot of us Americans are giving up the big cars — reluctantly in most cases. But they eat petrol and, apart from on long journeys, they aren't really necessary.'

My uncle pushed a button and a cold front of air filled the car.

'Air conditioning,' he explained through the mirror. 'It's essential when it gets really hot.'

I stared out of the window at the passing scenery. Everything looked so huge — the road . . . the cars . . . the whole skyline seemed larger than life!

'What time is it?' I asked, suddenly aware that my watch said nine o'clock at night which was crazy because it was broad daylight.

'Just about ten in the morning of your yesterday,' my uncle told me. 'And if that doesn't make sense, don't bother about it. Just accept it that it's still the tenth of July and we'll stop in a moment and have some American-style breakfast before we drive on home.'

'How far's that?' I asked.

'Not very far, honey,' Marcia said. 'It'll take us about two hours.'

'And that's not far?'

My uncle and aunt laughed. 'Not by American standards it's not,' Marcia told me.

'In that case, what's considered far?' I asked.

'Well, that's for you to judge, Carol.' My uncle indicated that he was turning off to the right and positioned himself in the four-lane traffic to pull off the main road. 'As a matter of fact, we've got quite an itinerary mapped out for you which we hope will show you just how big, big is. But right now it's time for some ham and eggs and my favourite hash brownies.'

I wondered what hash brownies were, and decided to take a risk and try them. After all, I was in America, wasn't I?

They turned out to be delicious. A sort of mashed potatoes and vegetables pattie fried till the outside was golden and crispy.

'Like to try one of my waffles with your eggs, Carol?' Marcia offered. 'I ordered a whole stock so there'd be plenty to go round. I know your uncle always steals one — so I ordered more than I can eat.'

'Well, if you're sure,' I said, eyeing the pile of delicious-looking latticed waffles.

'I'm sure,' she said, smiling, and placed two on my plate. 'Do you like maple syrup with them?' She went to pass me a small jug.

I winced. 'Er, not with my eggs, thanks,' I said and I guess my reaction must have shown because they both laughed.

'Don't worry, honey,' Marcia said, kindly, 'we Americans sure have some strange habits when it comes to what foods we mix together. You'll get used to it, though.'

I smiled and cut into a buttered waffle. For the life of me I couldn't ever imagine enjoying sweet syrup with ham and eggs! Yuk!

When we'd finished our giant-sized breakfasts, Uncle Richard paid at the check-out desk and held the door open for Marcia and me to leave.

The girl cashier smiled brightly as we walked past. 'You all have a good day, now,' she called after us.

I smiled back. 'And you!' I said, then couldn't understand why the smile vanished and a look of total confusion appeared.

I turned to my Uncle. 'Did I say something wrong?' I asked.

'Well, I guess it wasn't wrong, Carol,' he said, 'just sort of unusual. Wishing someone a good day here is like you saying thank you in Britain. You don't usually turn round after being served and say thank you back, do you?'

I thought about that for a while. It was true I suppose, but somehow it spoilt the effect. The girl had sounded so genuine and it seemed sad to think that what she'd said was just a routine response.

I shrugged, then skipped ahead to catch up with Marcia who was already by the car.

'You'll get used to lots of odd things here in America', she said cheerfully. 'And like it, too.'

'But I do already!' I said, breathing in the clear air . . . the brilliant sunshine. Everything looked brighter, bigger, more exciting. Oh, boy! I thought. You wait till I tell you about this, Claire and Becky, you'll eat your hearts out!

Chapter 8

Two hours and a million exciting, thrilling miles later we turned off Highway Seventeen. One moment we were zooming along listening to an old Tammy Wynette melody and singing along with it and then my uncle turned on his indicator, checked his rear view mirror and swung the Dodge up a small unmade track. We came to a scrunching halt an inch away from an enormous pair of iron gates.

'Here we are,' he announced, turning to grin at me. 'Home sweet home.'

I stared ahead. All I could see was the track disappearing between some enormous trees – but no house.

'The house is about a quarter of a mile further up the mountain,' Marcia explained. She turned to her husband. 'I'll fix the gates,' she told him.

'Okay, but be careful of that poison ivy,' my uncle called as Marcia jumped out and headed for the gates.

'What's poison ivy?' I asked. It sounded horrible.

'Look, see that climbing plant over by the gate — the one with the very dark foliage?' I nodded. 'Well, that's poison ivy.'

'Does it poison you?' I asked.

'Not exactly, but if it touches your skin you can break out in a very nasty rash and it can be painful. We don't have a lot of it round the place, but keep your eyes open just in case, okay?'

'You bet!' I didn't like the sound of it one bit!

Marcia stood by the open gates as we drove through and stopped on the far side. Then she closed them and clambered back into the car.

'Okay, let her roll!' she ordered, emulating the call used in the old wagon trains which pioneered the West.

I laughed. Marcia was good fun. I'd only met her less than three hours ago and yet I felt as if I'd known her for years. From what I could remember, she wasn't as elegant or as beautiful as Uncle Richard's first wife, Stella — but she was a whole lot more human. I suddenly had a great desire to meet Marcia's sons because, I decided, if they were anything like their mother, they too were going to be fun!

'Those are the famous redwood trees,' my uncle pointed out as we drove up the track to the house. 'This whole area is known as redwood country. It's been said that some of these trees are the oldest living things in the world. Aren't they magnificent?'

I stared at the mighty trees towering up and up. I

craned my neck to try and see the tops, but I couldn't. I had never seen trees so tall or wide.

'We mean to take you to Muir Woods on a trip,' Marcia said. 'You'll love it. There's a tree there with the entire centre burned out. Naturalists say it must have happened over a thousand years ago and yet the shell of the tree is still alive today.'

I shook my head in amazement and made a mental note to put all the information I could about the redwoods in my project.

Uncle Richard honked the horn as we drove up to the front of a single-storey, ranch-style house. It was made of redwood logs and blended in so well with the hillside that at first glance it didn't look very big at all – but then I saw that it extended way back and had two wings at either end – rather like an E with the middle bit missing. All along the long section was a wooden veranda. It overlooked the hillside, which dipped down to a magnificent valley.

At the sound of the car horn, two massive German shepherd dogs pounded out of the woods and started jumping up at the car windows, barking and wagging their tails like mad.

'The larger one is the dog – he's Caesar,' called Marcia above the barking. 'The bitch is Cleo. Not very original but the best the boys could dream up at the time.'

At that moment, as we climbed out of the car, accompanied by even more yapping and barking, a young copper-haired boy came running round the side of the house, waving frantically.

'Hi, Richard! Mom!'

I decided this had to be Paul Junior. He had the same round, mobile face as his mother, and bright brown eyes. And when he smiled, as he did when he shook my hand, dimples appeared in his cheeks.

'Hey, you're big!' Paul said, grinning sheepishly.

'And you're not wearing nappies!' I countered. He looked up at his mother, puzzled.

'What are nappies, Mom?' he asked.

'What babies wear – diapers,' his mother explained.

'Why should I be wearing diapers?' he asked, screwing up his face, bewildered.

'Because I thought you would be much younger,' I said, wishing I'd never opened my mouth.

Paul stared at me for a moment, obviously trying to decide if I was crazy or something. He must have decided I was okay because he snapped his fingers. 'I get it!' he said. 'Like I got to believe you were little – you thought I was a baby, right?'

'Stop that chattering and make yourself handy, lad,' uncle Richard said from the hatch-back. Then added, 'That's if you can manage this great big heavy case.' He said it challengingly and Paul Junior rose to the bait.

'I'm stronger than you are!' he boasted and ran over to relieve his step-father of my luggage.

'Come on, let's leave the men to it,' Marcia said,

taking my elbow and leading me towards the front door.'

'Where's Chuck?' I asked, wondering when her eldest son would make an appearance.

'Probably out in the woods, knowing him,' Marcia said. 'There's deer around here, and some interesting species of birds – Chuck's sort of keen on wild life. But he'll be in later, when he gets hungry. And that's very often.'

I smiled wanly, somehow feeling disappointed. I followed Marcia through a spacious sitting-room with a quarry-stone fireplace on one side, and beautiful bright orange-and-red Spanish-style rugs scattered over the polished parquet flooring. Inside the house, like outside, everything seemed so much larger than at home. The long sofa could easily seat five people – and there were two of them, one either side of the fireplace! Even the easy chairs looked big enough for two people to sit on. The house smelled of furniture polish and the dry, musky smell of geraniums which stood in pots along the empty fireplace, and on shelves by the windows.

Marcia caught me looking at them. 'I have to bring them in or the deer and the gerbils eat the lot!' she explained.

'Gerbils?' I asked.

'Yep! They're lovely little things but they play havoc with the garden!'

We walked down a short passage which ran off the living area, past two doors which, Marcia told me, were Chuck's and Paul Junior's dens, to a door at the end. She opened it, then stood back to let me through.

The bedroom was so pretty it took my breath away. It reminded me of one of those rooms you only see in house-and-garden type magazines. The whole décor was done in green and white – tiny flowered curtains and matching bedcover. Built-in wall-to-wall wardrobes and a cool olive-green carpet. Scatter cushions and two bedside rugs were the only contrasting colour and they were in a sunny yellow – the exact colour of the arrangement of flowers which stood reflected in the dressing-table mirror.

'I hope this is going to be okay for you,' Marcia said.

'Okay? It's beautiful!' I turned and beamed at her. 'And the flowers – that's a lovely thought. Thank you.'

Marcia's eyes twinkled. 'It's a pleasure to be able to add feminine touches for once,' she confessed. 'With a house full of men, I don't often get the chance. Sometimes I get the impression that we're all lads together. Believe me it can get very confusing. I have to keep reminding myself of my identity.' She laughed. 'To tell you the truth, I can't remember the last time I wore a skirt. It's getting to be serious.'

She grinned and walked over to the wardrobes. 'Look here,' she said. She held a handle of one of the sections. 'What do you see?' she asked.

Puzzled, I said, 'A wardrobe?'

Pleased at her deception she swiftly pulled it open to reveal a compact shower room, complete with toilet and washbasin. 'Tra la!' she cried. 'See what we have hidden behind. Neat, eh?'

'Fantastic!' I replied, admiring the green-and-white tiling and green fitments.

'Well – it's all yours while you're here,' Marcia said, turning round and walking back into the room, just as Paul staggered in with both my suitcase and holdall.

'Where do you want your bags, ma'am?' Paul asked, mimicking a porter in a hotel.

I latched on to the charade. 'Over there, my good man,' I said in a posh London accent.

Laughing, Paul staggered a bit further, then dropped the bags where he stood, puffing and panting. In his cut-off jeans and Crazy Horse sleeveless tee-shirt, he looked all arms and legs.

'I sure don't know what you're carrying in those, but I'm surprised the plane managed to get off the ground!' he said.

I knew what he meant. I'd packed everything – just in case! But now, I had a feeling most of the clothes would stay packed. Casual clothes seemed to be the norm around the house. Not that I minded because I'm happier in casual wear anyway.

'I've got a suggestion to make,' Marcia said walking over to the doorway. 'Say no if you don't like it, okay?' I nodded, waiting. 'I suggest you have a shower, freshen up and then, unless you're starving, why not take a nap until this afternoon? I should imagine you're still a bit disorientated and probably tired. I'll wake you up later and then you can get dressed and we'll make a barbecue out on the deck.'

I nodded. 'Sounds good to me,' I said, loving the idea of changing out of my crumpled clothes which I seemed to have been wearing for days!

'Okay – have fun,' she said. 'We'll see you later.' She turned to leave, then stopped and turned back. 'Oh, by the way,' she added. 'Welcome to the Walker madhouse. I want you to know I think it's great your coming here.'

I didn't know what to say, so I just smiled and said, 'Thank you.'

'My pleasure, Carol,' she said, sincerely, then turned and left me.

I stood for a moment staring at the closed door. She was really great. Super. More like a sister than a mother, I thought. Then I turned and started stripping off my hot, sticky skirt and blouse, my light-weight bra, and panties. With each piece of clothing came a feeling of wonderful relief. Finally, naked, I walked into the shower room, discovered how the mixer taps worked, and finally stood under a jet of cooling, tepid water. It was the nearest thing I'd known to Heaven.

There were some bottles on the shelf under the shower taps. I picked one up with 'shampoo' written on it and poured a small amount into my palm. As I lifted it to my hair, I smelled almond blossom – it was lovely. The blossomy smell grew stronger as I rubbed the gel into a mass of suds in my hair. I closed my eyes, feeling slightly unreal. Dizzy. It was hard to believe I was really here, standing under a shower, washing my hair in California!

It was too much. All my worries and fears about coming ... of meeting my uncle again — and of meeting Marcia and her children — seemed so far away. So stupid!

I rinsed off the shampoo then stood under the water until my hair felt squeaky clean. After a few more minutes, reluctantly, I turned off the water and reached for the bath towel.

As I dried myself I suddenly felt terribly tired. I couldn't even be bothered to dry my hair with the hair dryer I'd discovered on the vanity unit by the handbasin.

So I took the hand-towel and swirled it round my head turban-fashion, then draping the bath wrap round me I walked through, bare-footed, to the pretty bedroom. The bed looked so inviting, and my eyelids felt so heavy. . . .

A sudden movement outside the window caught my attention. I wandered over, drew back the net curtains and looked out. The view was to the side of the house, overlooking the Redwoods. The massive trees crowded close to the house, but a little way off I could see a clearing. The movement had been caused by a deer. I saw it dappled in the watery sunlight in the clearing. It stood under the overhanging branches of the trees, its head held at an angle on its slim, elegant neck. The animal's eyes — great black pools — seemed to search the undergrowth. Its ears twitched, listening. Every muscle in the delicately defined body was pulled taught. Expectant. And then with one graceful leap it had cleared the area and had disappeared into the depths of the woods.

I stood transfixed by the natural beauty of the scene I had just witnessed. I had seen deer plenty of times before in Richmond Park but they were tame and somehow couldn't match the splendour of the animal in its natural surroundings. I was enchanted by it.

And then I saw the reason why the deer had fled. He came into the clearing, treading carefully over fallen branches and undergrowth, carrying an expensive-looking camera in his hands. He was tall, well over six feet, I guessed, with a shock of copper-coloured hair which glinted in the shafts of sunlight filtering through the trees. He was dressed casually in army drill trousers and a khaki-coloured shirt. He stared in the direction the deer had fled; then, as I was watching, he turned and we were staring at each other. For one awful, embarrassing moment I didn't know what to do. Run and hide, or stand still and pretend I didn't care?

The boy raised a hand and waved at me, a grin creasing his tanned, handsome face.

I raised my hand to wave back and just as I did, two things happened. The boy raised his camera to take a picture – and the towel I had been wearing fell to the floor.

It was followed immediately by me! But not before I noticed the look of total disbelief in a pair of blue eyes and then the sudden slight movement of the finger poised over the camera.

On hands and knees I crawled over the floor and frantically clambered between the clean sheets.

I felt so ashamed. So embarrassed!

I'd met Chuck all right – and in a way neither of us would ever forget!

Chapter 9

Marcia woke me with a glass of orange juice at six o'clock Californian time. I gave up trying to work out what time it was back in England. All that filled my head was having to meet Chuck face to face after the embarrassing incident through the window.

'Dress casually,' Marcia said, then added, 'the only time we ever dress up is when we go into San Francisco or are invited out somewhere special. So don't feel you have to pretty yourself up too much around the house.'

I smiled and thanked her for the drink. But I died inside when I thought about dressing casually. How more casual can you get than wearing nothing!

And what made it worse was the thought that it was actually on film! Surely Chuck wouldn't be that mean? He'd have to destroy it, wouldn't he?

I slipped out of bed and sorted through my case, deciding what to wear. I opted for a pair of white shorts and an orange tee-shirt I'd bought in Carnaby Street. It was sleeveless and had a scooped neckline. I looked at myself in the full-length mirror I'd found inside one of the wardrobe doors and got cold feet. It was too revealing — and that's the last thing I wanted for my face-to-face meeting with Chuck.

I ended up wearing a pair of pink-striped dungarees over a cream cotton-knit top. I tied my long hair high on top of my head and slipped on my new thong sandals. Then, feeling confident and sure of myself, I walked out to the deck at the back of the house where I could hear a lot of chatter and occasional bursts of laughter.

The smell of charcoal filled the air; the sun slanted low from across the valley, bathing the tree tops and house in a soft rosy glow.

'Hey, so there you are,' my uncle greeted me. He was holding a long pronged fork, on the end of which dangled a juicy steak. 'Did you sleep well?'

'Yes, thanks,' I replied.

'Help yourself to a drink,' Marcia said, indicating a table by the kitchen door which was laden with an assortment of bottles. 'There's plenty of everything, so don't be shy. Oh, and the ice is in the freezer.'

'Do you like root beer?' Paul asked, as I approached the table where he was busy concocting a multi-coloured drink in a long glass.

'I've never tried it,' I said, then added, 'but I don't like alcohol anyway.'

Paul laughed, showing his braced teeth. 'It isn't alcoholic, silly! You mean you've never tried MacDonalds' famous root beer with your hamburger?'

Marcia passed on her way to the kitchen. 'Try it, Carol,' she said. 'We drink it a lot over here.'

When in Rome, I thought, and looked for the bottle.

'I'll pour it,' Paul offered. 'You have to be careful otherwise it all froths up and you get a glass full of froth and no drink.'

'Okay, thanks,' I said, and wandered back to the far end of the wooden veranda to stand by my uncle who was in charge of cooking the meat. The smoke wafted up on the cool night air, mingling with the tangy smell of the pines. Somewhere in the nearby thicket a bird trilled loudly, gnats buzzed and cicadas joined in with their chirruping. I breathed in deeply, feeling the softness of the night creeping in around the house. It was magical.

It's just like another world, I thought, trying to compare it with our semi near Wimbledon Common. But try as I might, I couldn't even conjure up the faintest outline of my home back in England.

'Is it a private daydream or can anyone join in?'

His voice shot my eyes open in an instance. He was standing not a foot from me, dressed as I'd seen him that afternoon. Only he wasn't carrying his camera this time.

'Meet big brother Chuck,' Paul said, coming over to hand me a frosted glass full of root beer.

'We've met already,' Chuck said, then grinned, 'well, almost, right?' He let his eyes wander over my dungarees down to my sandals and then slowly up again. With every inch, I felt my colour deepening in my cheeks. By the time his pale eyes met mine I felt myself blushing to the roots of my hair.

Paul had walked away, down to watch my uncle cook the steaks, so Chuck and I were left alone. I decided to be bold.

'I believe you have something which belongs to me?' I said, coldly.

One eyebrow shot up in his handsome face. 'Oh?'

His pretence was making me nervous and usually when I get nervous I get cross, too.

'Don't pretend you don't know what I'm talking about,' I said. 'The photo you took this afternoon – I'd like the negative.'

'Would you?' He was playing with me, teasing, and that really got me.

'Look, Chuck, what happened was unfair – and you took advantage of the situation. So let's not be silly. Let me have the film. I'll pay for a new one.'

'But how can you possibly pay for all the marvellous shots I've taken today? No, I'm afraid its out of the question. And besides, I'm interested in nature. Beautiful things. So if you don't mind, I think I'll keep it.'

'Chuck!' I bit my tongue from saying what was on the tip of it because, at that moment, Marcia arrived holding a bowl of baked potatoes.

'Piping hot from the microwave,' she said, and

smiled. 'Boy! When I think how our forebears slaved over camp fires . . . I'd never have made a pioneer's wife.'

'Here let me, Mom,' Chuck said and lifted the bowl from her. He glanced back over his shoulder. 'Come on, Carol,' he called. 'Come and see how we Yanks like to eat. None of your fancy silverware and table linen for us. We like everything basic – no fuss. Back to nature sort of thing, right Mom?'

'Well, I wouldn't go as far as to say that . . .' she said.

But I wasn't listening to what Marcia was saying – I was staring daggers after Chuck, smarting under his teasing tone.

Somehow, I thought, I'll get even with you, Mr Smarty! But for the moment, it would have to wait.

And anyway, the fact was that with all the fresh air and the succulent smell of barbecued meat, I was suddenly starving. I tried to think when I'd last eaten – but it was all jumbled up. I'd had breakfast, of course, but by British time that was probably my dinner. Then I thought that was crazy because that would mean I'd be having two dinners on the same day – only on opposite sides of the Atlantic.

'Come on, Carol, take a plate,' my uncle said, handing me one. 'And don't wait for us to have to ask you what you want. Just tuck in and help your-self. After all, you are family.'

I smiled over at him, as he stood perspiring by the open fire. A black smudge crossed his forehead where he'd wiped it with his arm. He was dressed in a pair of old shorts and a tee-shirt – complete with a striped butcher's apron – and looked more like an overgrown boy scout than a pilot. He certainly didn't look old enough to be flying planes.

I wanted to ask how old he was but didn't because I thought it would be rude. Still, trying to calculate it from Mum's age – and she's thirty-six – I made him about thirty-two.

That meant he was five years younger than Dad. I thought about that for a while as I chewed on my steak. And I had to admit, reluctantly, that compared to Uncle Richard, Dad seemed old.

It has to be this outdoor type of life, I thought. The getting back to nature bit. Oh, damn – I thought, remembering Chuck's photo – all this thinking it getting me nowhere.

I glanced over to where Chuck sat on the railing of the deck, one leg dangling, his eyes lost in a faraway gaze, as he studied the spectacular sunset. For a moment I forgot about the photo and his teasing remarks and just stared at him. His profile was perfect – in fact everything about him was perfect. It occurred to me then that he was probably the best-looking boy I'd ever seen.

And the thought of it brought a hot flush to my cheeks. Whatever was I thinking of? He was horrible! He had a photograph of me which he should never have taken – let alone keep!

Remembering this made me glare across at him. At that moment, he chose to turn and look in my direction. When he smiled, I forget what I was angry

about. And to my astonishment, I found myself
smiling back!

Chapter 10

'Chuck and Paul are going to take you to the beach,
Carol,' Marcia said, after we had breakfasted on corn
muffins and crispy bacon rashers. 'That's if you like
swimming?'

'I love it!' I said, enthusiastically. I stared out the
window. High above the giant trees the sky was an
unbelievable blue, with not a cloud in sight.

'How about surfing?' Paul asked.

My heart sank. 'Surfing?'

It was Chuck who came to my rescue. 'Don't
worry, we won't throw you in at the deep end. If
you want to learn I'll teach you. If not, you can enjoy
watching the rest of us – most of the other girls just
stay on the beach looking decorative, so you won't
be alone.'

'Oh?' I didn't think I liked the idea of being part
of a pin-up parade for the local Romeos. So I said,
'I'd like to try it, if possible.'

'Good for you!' Marcia said, proudly. 'That's what
I like, a girl with spirit. Show the fellas we're not the
weaker sex, right?'

'Right!' I agreed, but my voice didn't sound very convincing even to my ears. 'Who are these "others" you mention?' I asked Chuck.

'Oh, just a crowd of kids from round here – and a few who spend the holidays here in rented houses along the beach,' he replied.

'Where are you going?' my uncle asked, coming into the dining area from the kitchen.

Chuck shrugged. 'Haven't decided,' he replied. 'But I guess it's all right if I borrow one of the cars, isn't it?'

'Depends,' my uncle said.

'On?' Chuck turned to watch his step-father walk over to the window.

When he turned to face Chuck, he was grinning. 'Who's paying for the gas?' he asked.

Chuck's face fell. 'Aw, come on, Richard,' he said, 'you know I don't get my allowance until the end of the month and I spent most of this month's on that new long-distance lens for my camera.'

His words brought the photo back into my mind – not that it was ever very far away.

'I've got some money –' I began.

'And you hold on to it,' Marcia said, wagging a finger at me. 'Don't you let me hear you've been spending money on outings with Chuck. I'm all for equality – but not when you're a guest here. No, this young man's got to learn the value of money and he won't do it by spending everything at the beginning of the month and then subbing for the rest of the time.'

'Okay, okay!' Chuck said, raising his hands as if to ward off a blow. 'We'll walk down through the woods – Carol will enjoy it anyway, as she's expressed a delight in nature.' He shot me a look which sent my blood boiling. 'And then we'll come back with one of the others – maybe stop off at Los Gatos and show her some of the local landmarks.'

Marcia looked at her husband and I saw them exchange meaningful glances.

'Okay, okay,' my uncle suddenly said. 'You can use the Honda – but I want it back with the tank re-filled, okay?'

'Sure,' Chuck agreed. 'No sweat.' He jumped up and began heading for his bedroom which was next to mine. 'Well come on then, you two, if you're coming,' he called over his shoulder. 'Let's make tracks.'

I glanced across at Marcia, who was shaking her head. 'Don't take any nonsense from that one,' she said. 'I sometimes think he needs to be kept in tow by a strong-minded woman. He gets too much his own way.'

'It's his incredible good looks and charm that do it,' Paul said, really laying it on. Then added. 'Just like me.'

'Get out!' his mother said, threateningly.

'Can I give you a hand with clearing the dishes?' I asked.

'Good Heavens, no. But thanks for the offer. I let Jackson do all that.'

'Jackson?' I asked, thinking perhaps she had a man in to help.

Marcia laughed and the dimples appeared. She jabbed a finger over her shoulder to the kitchen area.

'He's the one between Mrs Malloy, the washing machine, and Dr Johnson, my spin dryer.'

I shook my head, totally confused, and Marcia laughed.

'Jackson's the dishwasher, sweetie,' she said. 'I wouldn't be without it.'

I gazed at the alignment of machines standing to attention along the kitchen walls — it was a bit like being in an electricity showroom back home. The kitchen seemed to boast everything from a multiple toaster to the microwave oven. And included in the range was an automatic yoghurt maker, soda fountain, magi-mix and a double oven! Compared with Mum's kitchen back home, this looked as if it belonged to another world!

'Do you need a swimsuit?' Marcia asked.

I shook my head, 'No thanks, I've got two with me.'

Marcia laughed. 'I don't know why I asked that,' she said. 'I hardly think mine would fit you, you've got such a lovely slim figure. But I'll get you a beach towel and there's a bag you can take which usually holds all the beach gear.'

'Aren't you and Uncle Richard coming?' I asked.

My uncle looked up from the letters he'd been reading. 'Sorry, pet,' he said, 'but I'm due down at

69

the airport today. It's the day I put in my bids for what flights I want next month.'

'Oh.' I turned to Marcia. 'Why don't you join us?' I asked. But she shook her head.

'I've got a gadget to do just about everything but unfortunately they haven't invented a robot yet which can be programmed to select what shopping I want and then go choose the best.'

'Don't worry, Marcia, honey,' my uncle said, winking over at me, 'we're working on it.'

Just at that moment Chuck and Paul came bursting back into the room.

'Ready?' Chuck asked me.

Marcia scowled at her son. 'Don't be so impatient,' she scolded him. 'What's the hurry?'

'I don't want all the best breakers to be used up before I get there.' Chuck grinned.

I stood up and walked round him. 'Won't be a moment,' I said. 'I'll just change into my costume and grab my bag.'

'You'd better bring a book with you,' he called after me. Then added, 'You might be bored!'

He had to be joking! Me bored? On a beach in California. . . ? It suddenly occurred to me that he must mix with an odd bunch of girls if they were bored that easily.

I slipped on my new mini bikini, and stuffed my spare one into the special polythene bag my Mum had packed. Then I put my new cotton beach wrap with it. When I went back out, everyone seemed to be at the front of the house.

As I arrived on the scene, Marica handed me a large, brightly striped beach bag which had the words BIG BAG picked out in contrasting colours on the stripes. 'The towels and suntan creams are in there,' she told me. 'And be careful you don't get burned.'

'I won't,' I said, taking the bag and dropping my own things into it.

Chuck backed the gold coloured Honda out of the garage at the side of the house, and stopped by the front door to allow Paul and me to climb in.

'Have yourselves a good time!' Marcia called, and in reply, Chuck honked the horn which in turn started Caesar and Cleo barking and running after us.

I peered out the back window. My uncle was standing behind Marcia, his hands on her shoulders, and the dogs were bounding up to them. Behind them the house looked homely and impressive. But more impressive still were the gigantic redwoods towering over the house.

Sitting back in the seat, I sighed.

'Tired?' Chuck asked, watching me through the mirror, a glint in the depths of his blue eyes.

I smiled smugly back at him. 'Not yet,' I said. 'But don't worry, I'll let you know when I am.'

Paul Junior slid down in the passenger seat next to his brother and pushed his straw hat further down over his forehead, obscuring his face.

'Oh, heck!' he said from the depths of his seat. 'Looks like big brother Chuck has done it again!'

'Done what?' I asked, puzzled.

'Rubbed a girl up the wrong way,' Paul answered, peering at me from under his hat, liberally festooned with fishing flies.

'Oh,' I said suddenly interested, 'does he manage to do that often?'

Paul laughed and sat up straight. 'Often? That's a joke! He does it every time! What I can't understand is why the girls keep coming back for more. Especially when I'm around.'

I reached forward and pushed the hat back down over his face.

'Well, believe me – I'm not impressed,' I said. Involuntarily my eyes looked up into the driving mirror. I knew it was the last thing I should have done because the moment our gazes met, Chuck winked at me. And it wasn't a quick, cheeky type of wink. It was a very slow, calculated one which sent goose-pimples racing up my spine.

'That reminds me, Chuck,' I said, trying to keep the venom from my voice, 'we still have some unfinished business to talk about.'

He gave a short laugh. 'What business?' he asked, infuriatingly, pretending to concentrate on driving along the freeway. 'As far as I'm concerned there isn't any.'

'I could pay you for your – er ... troubles,' I cajoled. Adding, 'It would help you out till the end of the month.'

'A person could get the wrong impression hearing you say things like that, you know,' Chuck said, sounding 'holier than thou'.

I bit my lip and stared out the window. He was impossible!

'Nearly there,' Paul informed me as Chuck turned the car off the highway and headed down a secondary road. 'Look there, see, through the gap in the trees – that's the mighty Pacific.'

I stared ahead and saw it. A strip of indigo against the lighter blue of the sky. And in front of it was a wide strip of silver sand.

Chuck swung the car into an area marked *Beach Parking Lot* and applied the brakes. I braced myself against his seat to stop myself shooting forward.

'Everybody out,' he instructed, throwing open his door and jumping down.

Before I could open my door, it jerked open. 'Allow me,' Chuck said, holding out a hand to assist me. I chose to ignore him and stepped down on to the hot concrete, turning my back to him. Undeterred, he slammed the door shut and hurried round to get the bags out of the boot.

He had just handed mine to me, when someone shouted my name.

Stunned, I blinked around in the strong sunlight to see who it was.

'Over here, Carol!'

I focused my eyes on a bright red sports car and recognized Louisa.

'How come you know Lou?' Chuck asked, staring at me.

'We met on the plane – she was with her mother. Why?'

73

'That's just our luck,' Paul said, turning his back towards the red car.

Puzzled, I looked back to where Lou was standing — only this time she wasn't alone. With her, and walking in our direction, was a tall, willowy blonde. She was wearing the briefest shorts I had ever seen and a figure-hugging halter top.

I stared from the strikingly beautiful girl to Chuck and then back again, and then I twigged.

'Another of your rare birds?' I asked, sweetly.

Give Chuck his due, he did colour up slightly. But then his square jawline tightened and the pale, teasing eyes were glinting again with good humour.

'She's not such a rare species as some I've caught on film,' he said, meeting my gaze.

'Hello, Chuck,' a deep husky voice said.

The tall elegant blonde seemed to ignore the fact that I was even present. But Lou came up and started talking to me.

'Are you coming to the beach, too?' she asked.

'Sure am,' I said. 'I want to learn to surf-ride.'

At that, Lou's sister turned to stare at me. I could feel her eyes summing me up, from my thong sandals to my white sundress. She smiled and I could see her mother's likeness, the same perfect teeth, the delicate chiselled bone structure. Only, of course, Mary Jo was older and certainly not as beautiful as her daughter.

'I'll teach you how to surf-board,' she said sweetly. 'Even if I say it myself, I'm the best girl surfer round here.'

'Don't bother yourself, Danielle,' Chuck cut in. 'I'm sure you've got a whole heap of things to do and people you have to see down on the beach.'

Danielle turned to smile at Chuck. 'Well, as a matter of fact, I have,' she said. 'But I was only trying to be friendly.'

'Thanks anyway,' I said, feeling I was watching some sort of private drama being enacted before me, or was it a tragedy?

If Danielle heard me, she didn't acknowledge what I had said. She kept looking with her large lavender eyes at Chuck who said nothing. So she turned to call Lou and continued on her way.

'Just another girl you rubbed up the wrong way?' I asked Chuck, snidely, watching him watching her sway down to the beach.

Chuck shook his head. 'Nope!' he said, grinning. And when I looked surprised, he added, 'She's the one who rubbed *me* up the wrong way.' Then before I could question him, he took the beach bag off me and started striding towards the beach.

I stood for a moment feeling sensations of fury and frustration surging through me. Who did he think he was, ordering me around? I looked around for some moral support from Paul, but he'd already started running after Chuck and, rather than be left stranded in the parking lot, I began reluctantly to follow.

By the time I reached the beach, Chuck had already laid out our towels by an overhang of rocks and was heading in the direction of the area where the surf boards were housed in long huts.

I stripped down to my bikini and arranged myself on one of the towels. All around me were golden-limbed girls and bronzed boys. Next to them, I felt like a peeled prawn! Still, I thought, I had to start somewhere. I dug out the suntan oil and managed to cover all of me except the centre of my back.

I thought about asking Chuck to help me, but pride coupled with a prude streak stopped me. I looked around for Paul, but he had gone off with a group of other boys to the far end of the beach. There was nothing else for it but to grin and suffer and make sure I kept that part of my back in the shade.

Chuck returned about fifteen minutes later, carrying a surf board with the stars and stripes painted on the top side. He towered over me, his well-proportioned body silhouetted by the sun, casting a shadow.

'Well, come on then,' he said, none too kindly, 'let's see if we can make a surfer out of you.'

I felt intimidated by him — not to mention just a tiny bit frightened of the enormous breakers which were rolling in.

'I think I'll take the sun for a while,' I said, 'if you don't mind.'

'Why should I mind?' Chuck replied. 'If you're scared —'

I jumped up. 'Who says I'm scared?'

His stern look melted. 'Now that's more like the girl I met yesterday,' he said, running his eyes over my brief, gold-coloured bikini.

I turned away from him and began striding down

the beach. As I neared the water's edge I turned back defiantly. 'Are you coming, or not?' I shouted.

'You can't go without me,' Chuck shouted back.

'No? Just watch!' I cried. Without thinking, I waded into the surf. It was freezing against my sunwarmed skin but I kept walking out, ignoring the cries which were coming to me from the beach.

What happened next, I'm not quite sure, but one moment I was standing up, knee deep in swirling water, and the next I was thrown upside down and found my chin on the sandy sea bed! I opened my eyes and looked through green water. The air seemed to be squeezed from my lungs and I remember thinking, 'What a way to end a holiday!'

A pair of strong hands started hauling me up . . . and up. My head suddenly broke the water and I gulped in air. I felt sick and weak, and very happy that I was being carried back to the safety of the sand.

I guess I must have passed out for a second because when I opened my eyes again I was lying on the wet sand and something warm and moist was being pressed against my lips. I tried to look up, but something was blocking my view and pressing me back down.

I clenched my fists and pushed as hard as I could.

'What did you do that for?' Chuck asked, looking angrily down at me from the kneeling position he had by my head.

'Me? What the heck do you think you were doing?' I demanded.

'Giving you the kiss of life, for God's sake!'

'Well, it might have escaped your attention that I'm not dead!' I shouted at him.

Someone nearby laughed huskily and it was then I realized there were several pairs of tanned feet standing around me.

I leaned on an elbow and, shading my eyes from the glare of the sun, squinted up pairs of legs to the sea of faces which peered down at me. In the front row, looking pityingly at where I lay sprawled on the sand, was Danielle.

'Hi!' I said. 'Lovely day, isn't it?'

She sniggered then, turning, pushed her way out of the crowd. Soon the rest of the feet wandered away, too. I lay back on the sand and tightly closed my eyes.

'Hey! You in there,' Chuck called. 'You okay?'

'I will be when you go away!' I replied through clenched teeth.

'Do you want to try again – only this time with a surf board?'

Boy! Was he a glutton for punishment. I opened one eye and fixed it on him. 'Go away!' I hissed.

He shrugged those perfect broad shoulders and stood up.

'Please yourself, lady,' he said. 'Only next time I'll let you drown.'

I sat up and watched him stride arrogantly down the beach towards the crowd of surfers who were standing watching a girl riding a giant roller. Whoever it was, she looked magnificent. Golden and agile and — and heck! I said out loud. As the sun caught her on the slant of the wave, it was as if she were under a spotlight. I might have known, I thought miserably, watching Danielle's perfect, graceful performance. It had to be Miss America herself!

You're jealous, I told myself. *I'm not*, a voice replied. *Then what are you?*

I thought that over for a while and finally conceded. I was jealous. Jealous of someone like Danielle — someone so poised and sure of herself. With such a perfect face and body. *Well, what are you going to do about it?* I asked myself. I sighed and started picking up lumps of wet sand, then letting them drop again. I didn't have an immediate answer. It was something I would have to think about. I rolled over on to my tummy and felt the sun warm on my back. I closed my eyes and pondered the question. Well, I thought as I let the sound of the waves lull me to sleep, I can start by allowing Chuck to teach me how to ride the rollers.

A soft breeze played against the skin of my back and I drifted off to sleep.

When I awoke, something was hurting. And then I remembered — my back. I hadn't had any suntan oil on it. I rolled over and sat up. My back was stinging like mad and when I tried to look over my shoulder, all I saw was a blur of bright pink.

So much for my surfing lessons! I wailed inwardly. And then I thought, I bet Danielle never suffers from sunburn.

I bet Danielle never suffers from anything!

Chapter 11

I spent the next two days of my holiday indoors with my back covered in some peculiar-smelling gel which, Marcia informed me, was an old Red Indian cure for sunburn.

'Are you an Indian?' I'd asked, impressed.

She laughed at that! 'Heavens no, honey! Nothing as exciting! I come from Italian descent.'

'Then how come you know about this gel?' I'd asked from my horizontal position on a sun bed on the shaded deck.

'I've a friend who owns a nature-cure shop downtown. She recommended it. It does work. You just have to be patient,' she assured me.

And it did work. It worked fantastically. After forty-eight hours my back wasn't sore at all. The only problem was I began to peel, and even I could see how ugly it looked and, let's face it, most of the time I wasn't in a position to see it! Still, I did as Marcia instructed and kept applying the greenish gel. After another two days, the peeling had stopped and I was left with a blotchy but possible tan.

'We thought we'd all fly down to Los Angeles this weekend,' my uncle informed me, over spare ribs and a green salad, and continued to say, 'spend a few days taking in the sights.'

'That sounds lovely,' I said. 'I've read quite a lot about it. Will we be able to visit Disneyland?'

'That's the idea,' Marcia said brightly. 'And I've

planned that we'll take in a trip round a few of the tourist attractions, too.' She handed me the plate of juicy spare ribs to help myself to some more – and I did. They were delicious.

'We'll fly down on Sunday – it will allow us time to go to Mary Jo's lawn party for Danielle and then if you kids want to stay over for a pool party on the Saturday, you can. That will still leave us time to be packed and ready to leave around Sunday noon.'

Everything sounded great – apart from the Danielle bit. I glanced over to Chuck to see if he'd reacted to it, but he was watching the dogs down below the deck, rolling round playing together.

It was Paul who spoke up. And I could have hugged him for it.

'Do we have to go to Danielle's lawn party, Mom?' he asked, his voice expressing as much enthusiasm as I felt.

Marcia looked surprised. 'Well, I think it's only fair,' she said, then glanced at Chuck. 'How do you feel about going?' she asked. Then added, 'After all, you and Danielle go back a long way.'

I wondered just what that meant, but decided it was one question I didn't really want to know the answer to.

Chuck stopped gazing at the dogs. 'I'm easy either way,' he said. 'But why not ask Carol? She's the one who'll maybe feel out of it. She doesn't even know anyone there.'

'Yes, she does,' Marcia said. 'She travelled over

with Mary Jo — it was really Carol she asked in the first place. I haven't kept in touch with Mary Jo, but now that she's made the effort I do feel we should make an appearance. What do you think, Richard?'

My uncle was concentrating on filling his pipe. 'What?' he asked, obviously unaware of the gist of the conversation.

'Do you think we ought to go to Mary Jo's lawn party, honey?'

My uncle nodded. 'Yes, I'd like to,' he said, definitely. 'Monte's a regular guy and we should begin to socialize as a family.'

I watched Marcia stand up and start collecting the dirty dishes for Jackson. 'Well, that's settled then,' she said, matter-of-factly. 'Chuck, you can give me a hand collecting the dishes, and Paul, run and get the angel cake out of the fridge.'

'Let me help,' I offered, about to stand up. But Marcia's hand gently eased me down.

'No, you stay here. Let the men try their hands at housework for a change. It won't hurt them. You can help by thinking up a nice surprise for Danielle's birthday present.'

I caught Chuck looking at me, a grin lighting his face as he read my thoughts . . . I had a hundred and one unique ideas for Danielle's birthday surprise but there wasn't one which I could mention to Marcia — and most of them weren't available in the shops!

'Don't go taxing that tiny brain of yours,' Chuck said, snidely, as he passed. 'I'm sure Danielle won't thank you!'

I smiled up at him. 'I know of something she *would* thank me for,' I said, sweetly.

'Oh?' he paused, interested.

'You. Gift-wrapped!' I said, low enough for my uncle not to hear.

If I expected that to rankle him, I was wrong. Because he matched my dazzling smile with his own.

'You're right, that's exactly what she wants for her birthday. How clever of you to have thought of it!'

I watched him walk into the kitchen and could have hit him. He was so . . . so . . . I searched frantically for the word. Conceited, I thought. And arrogant; just because he was tall, good-looking, clever, and could turn on the charm, he thought he was the answer to every girl's prayers.

Still, I thought desolately, he was probably right. Danielle *would* welcome him gift-wrapped. And by going to her party, he was all but offering her just that.

For a moment I wondered what she would be wearing, and then immediately dismissed the thought. Whatever she wore, she was going to look like someone out of Dallas! She was the type of girl who looked great in sackcloth and ashes!

Paul came back carrying a large platter with a magnificent white fluffy cake sitting on it.

'Wow!' I said, leaning over and peering at the frothy concoction. 'That looks magnificent. Did you make it, Marcia?'

'For once I can honestly say, yes. Making cakes is the one area where I shine. Don't ask me how. I just bung everything into my amazing multi-mix and put them into the micro, and hey-presto! Magic.'

I had to smile. Put like that, it sounded more as if Marcia were praising the art of mechanical cake-making rather than genuine gourmet cooking. But after tasting a slice of the mouth-melting angel cake, I decided I didn't care how it was made. It was delicious.

Chapter 12

There, I thought with satisfaction, that's quite a collection I've managed to get so far. I closed the folder marked PROJECT, and went to place it in my drawer for safe keeping.

My latest acquisition was a collection of lovely postcards of the redwoods, which I'd picked up from the lodge in Muir Woods National Park. I'd also bought a few presents to take home. The one I liked most was for Mum. It was a poem carved in a piece of highly polished wood. When I read it, especially the last verse about growing like the trees, 'straight, true and fine', I found a lump in my throat.

I'd been so lost in thought as I went on to read the lines saying 'God stands before you in these trees' that I'd physically jumped when Chuck slipped an arm round my shoulders.

'Makes you think, doesn't it?' he'd said, wistfully.

I'd nodded and let my eyes scan up and up till I was almost bending backwards to see the topmost branches. The fact that Chuck still had his arm along my shoulders didn't bother me until he said, 'Nothing like nature to turn you on is there?'

Catching the look in his eyes, I shrugged his arm off me. How could I forget, he still had my photograph!

The journey back from Muir Woods took us across the incredible Golden Gate Bridge – but I was really disappointed. It wasn't really golden at all. It was a dirty rust colour!

'Everyone's disappointed about that, Carol,' Uncle Richard told me, as he drove around to give me a quick tour of San Francisco. 'We'll spend a day here when we come back from LA,' he said as we drove past the beautiful church of St Peter and St Paul. Marcia had explained that we were driving through the historically famous Telegraph Hill in the North Beach area of the city.

'And that,' Paul Junior had pointed out, 'is Coit Tower. It's a memorial to the city's volunteer Fire Department.'

I'd stared at the towering monument. It rose like a giant concrete finger up into the blue Californian sky. It was so huge it seemed to dwarf even the twin spires of the church.

As we'd driven along Market Street, one of the

widest business streets in the world, so Chuck informed me, I saw my first cable car.

'I'll take you on a trip on one,' Chuck had offered. 'It's exciting, even if it is rather bumpy.'

'Yes, it is still one of the best ways of seeing over the city's hills, and it's great fun,' my uncle had said.

'It sounds fun,' I'd agreed.

'Right. Then that's a date,' Chuck had said, nicely.

It was only later that I questioned the decision. I mean about accepting his invitation. Still, I thought, as I placed some things of San Francisco in my folder, I'd worry about that when it came.

A soft knock on my door brought me back to the present.

'Yes?' I called. The door opened and Marcia put her head round.

'Reckon we've got about an hour before we have to make tracks for the party, Carol,' she said. She looked really pretty with her new bobbed hair.

'Okay,' I said. 'I'll start getting ready.'

'As you kids will be stopping over for the pool party tomorrow, don't forget to pack your swimsuit and sundress.'

'Oh, yes,' I said, a sinking feeling engulfing me. The idea of 'stopping over' went down like a lead ball. Mary Jo was okay, and little Lou was sweet, but big sister, Danielle – yuk!

Choosing what to wear was a problem. I'd never been to a garden party – or, as I'd learned it was called in America, a lawn party. All I'd ever heard about them were the ones the Queen gave at Buckingham Palace and somehow I didn't think hats and long gloves would go down very well in San José!

In the end I decided on my new white cotton sundress. Mum had chosen it, but I had to agree it was lovely. It was a simple sleeveless dress with a dropped waistline and high front. The cross-over back dipped daringly into a deep V which finally met to fasten with two small buttons at the dropped waistline.

It was impossible to wear a bra under it, but I didn't mind. It wasn't as if I had much of a bust-line anyway!

I slipped on my one and only pair of good sandals – two narrow strips of white leather which crisscrossed over my feet and tied around my ankles, then stood back and peered in the mirror, critically. I got quite a shock. The white of the dress emphasized just how tanned I was. I looked golden and healthy. I turned sideways to get a glimpse of how I looked from the back and saw that the deep V showed off my tan beautifully.

I swung my long newly shampooed hair off my face, then clipped on a pair of small silver rose earrings my parents had given me for Christmas. The earrings, and two thin silver bangles, were the only jewellery I wore.

When I walked out into the sitting-room, I felt great. Ready to meet a hundred Danielles.

'Wow! Hey, look ye here!' Uncle Richard exclaimed. 'Carol, you look as pretty as an angel!'

Marcia smiled, and sighed. 'Prettier. Boy, what

wouldn't I do to lose twenty years. Honey, you're a stunner!'

'You look great, too,' I told her, feeling embarrassed at the reaction I was getting.

Marcia looked down at her cream floaty dress and pulled a face. 'It hides the bumpy bits,' she said. 'And it's loose, so I can breathe.' She emphasized the last word and it made me laugh.

'Come on, you boys!' my uncle called down the passage.

'Just coming!' came Chuck's curt reply. He didn't sound at all happy and for a moment I wondered why he was so reluctant to go to Danielle's birthday party. Or maybe, I thought, he's just putting it on. Playing hard to get.

Hey, what do you care anyway? I asked myself.

I don't! came the reply.

If I'd held my breath waiting for Chuck to make some admiring remark about my outfit, let's face it, I'd be dead.

He ignored me. And that hurt. But I chose to do the same and ignore him.

The trip down to Mary Jo's mansion – that's what it turned out to be! – was oddly quiet at the back of the car, with me sandwiched between a brooding Chuck and a sullen Paul. Only Uncle Richard and Marcia didn't seem to notice. They spent the whole time pointing out local landmarks – like the orange and lemon groves in the valley, and the distant misty mountain ranges.

As we passed through San José to Mary Jo's home, I looked out and saw a peculiar, odd-angled house set back off the road.

'That's the Winchester Mystery House, Carol,' my uncle said, glancing over his shoulder as we stopped at a road junction. 'It has over a hundred and sixty rooms, two thousand doors – and thirteen bathrooms.'

'You're joking!' I exclaimed, peering back at the enormous, weird-shaped building.

'It's also got over ten thousand windows!' Marcia added. Then went on to explain, 'It was built by a very eccentric heiress – Sarah Winchester. She had that monstrosity designed to baffle the evil spirits which she believed haunted her.'

The lights changed down and we started moving again. I settled back between Chuck and Paul.

'She must have been a bit odd,' I remarked.

'Aren't all females?' Chuck said.

I was about to make a rude reply, but didn't.

And when he glanced across at me, obviously expecting me to comment, I really threw him – I smiled sweetly.

An hour after we had arrived at Mary Jo's and her husband Monte's palatial home, I wanted to go back to Los Gatos! Or even, for that matter, to Wimbledon. And it wasn't that anyone was nasty or rude, or anything like that. It was the fact that I obviously didn't fit in with the glittering, moneyed surroundings. In my cotton sundress, I stuck out like a sore thumb. Everybody seemed to be wearing what looked like expensive silk originals. Even the maids, in their neat black and white uniforms, looked elegant!

Also, apart from that, I didn't know anyone. I was welcomed sweetly and introduced around, but after a few polite enquiries about England, people's attention was directed elsewhere. Mary Jo and her husband greeted Uncle Richard and Marcia like the long lost friends they had been, and Mary Jo was insistent that she showed Marcia the new decorations in the house, while Monte directed my uncle to the new terraces he'd had built round the pool area.

I hadn't seen Chuck for about two seconds after we'd arrived – thanks to Danielle. And even Paul had been swallowed up by a group of other kids.

I clutched a glass of lemonade and wandered over the beautifully manicured lawns towards an artificial pond complete with lilipads. There was even an artificially built waterfall running into it. Next to the mouth of the waterfall stood a sort of summer house, shaped like a Grecian temple, and painted white.

Music drifted across the lawns. As I walked away from the guests the chattering voices faded until they were just a hum. I sipped the chilled lemon and wandered on; skirting the immaculate flower-beds, I found myself on a small stone path which led down to the pretty summer house which I could now see reflected in the pond.

On a sudden impulse I slipped off my sandals and, with them dangling in one hand, I began to walk over the deliciously cool springy grass. I had reached the summer house before I heard the voices.

I stood stock still, recognizing Danielle's husky tones.

'. . . thank you for coming,' she was saying, her deep voice even deeper with emotion. 'I didn't think you would, you were so cool to me the other day on the beach . . . and you shouldn't be because you know how I feel about you —' Her words stopped abruptly and I could just imagine Chuck pulling her into his arms and stopping her words with his kisses. The idea of it made me want to be sick!

Without stopping to hear more, I turned and started running back over the grass towards the house. As I came to the flower-beds and the path, I glared over my shoulder to the summer house, wondering if the secret lovers had heard me. No one had appeared so I continued to run away. Then as I rounded an oleander bush, I met a brick wall!

'Hey, watch out!' a familiar voice called. But it was too late. I lost my balance on the slippery stones and then I felt myself falling. . . .

When I surfaced, I was standing knee-deep in muddy water with bits of water lilies in my mouth and hair.

'The pool party isn't until tomorrow,' Chuck said, standing with his arms crossed over his broad chest. He was grinning from ear to ear.

I glared at him, then suddenly questioned how he could be standing there when he had been down in the summer house a few minutes earlier. I glanced back in the direction I had run and saw Danielle watching me, laughing. Beside her was a tall, dark-haired stranger who was also enjoying the water ballet!

I reached out a muddy hand. 'Don't just stand there,' I said. 'Help me out!'

Chuck didn't move. 'I thought you didn't need help from anyone!' he called back. 'Least of all a male!'

A wave of anger and humiliation swept over me.

'Chuck . . .' I wailed. 'Please?'

The amusement disappeared from his eyes and was replaced by a look of concern. He leaned forward, took my hands in his and unceremoniously hauled me out of the water and into the circle of his arms. Before I knew what was happening, he had bent his head and pressed his lips on to mine.

Frantically, I pushed away from him. 'I can't breathe,' I said, gulping air. Then, when I looked at him through my water-spiked lashes, I couldn't help the laughter bubbling up inside me.

'I don't see the joke,' Chuck said, a hurt, angry expression on his face. He'd obviously expected his kiss to have a different effect on me.

'I do!' I said, beginning to giggle. 'Just look at you!'

Chuck looked to where I was pointing. The whole front of his clean white shirt and slacks was streaked with slimy mud!

'Well, that sure settles it!' he stated, firmly, unamused.

'Settles what?' I asked, still finding the whole thing enormously funny.

'It settles the fact that we don't stay on for Danielle's pool party tomorrow. Boy, am I glad! I couldn't stand the idea of it. The last time she held one, she acted like a prima donna, flitting from one admiring male to another.'

'So that's it! You're jealous,' I said.

Chuck stared at me for a moment, then laughed drily. 'You really are very young,' he said and began walking away.

His words hit me like a slap in the face. Young, indeed. I was so angry I wanted to scream at him, but he'd disappeared round the oleander bushes. Pent-up and frustrated, I looked around for something to take my temper out on. In the distance Danielle was still watching me, smiling. Young, was I? Well, okay, Mr Clever Chuck Walker, I thought, if I'm that young I might as well enjoy it. And giving in to an impulse, I stuck my tongue out at Danielle. Just the look of shocked surprise on her beautiful face was worth my falling in her stupid lily pond.

Uncle Richard and Marcia somehow didn't seem particularly upset to have to leave the party early. Mary Jo had seemed more upset than anyone. But I think it was really to do with the state I was in when I reappeared on the scene looking like a stand-in for Nessie – the legendary Loch Ness monster.

'Oh, for Lord's sake!' she exclaimed. Then hurried

me away to the back of the house to change before too many of her guests were upset by the mess I presented on two legs.

I could just see what was going through her manicured mind. *Her* daughters would never turn up looking like something the dog dug up — then buried again!

I finished up driving back to Los Gatos in my bikini and sun wrap. Anything rather than the humiliation of borrowing one of Danielle's dresses!

Chapter 13

The trip down to Los Angeles was easy. Getting out of the John Wayne—Orange County airport was the hard part. It was a bit like the maze at Hampton Court, only a million times worse.

Just when Uncle Richard was about to abandon the hire car he had rented and set up camp in the airport's forecourt, Chuck had a brilliant idea.

'Follow that cab,' he said. 'A cabbie's bound to know his way out of this concrete rabbit-warren.'

It worked like magic — and fifteen minutes later we were crossing the San Diego freeway, heading for Disneyland.

'Phew!' my uncle exclaimed. 'No wonder the big

joke at the moment is that LA airport is in such a mess they are going to institute a new event in the Olympics — and grant a special medal for the person who can get from the airport to the Olympic grounds and back in the fastest time! That's if they can do it at all!'

'Hey, Richard,' Paul said, excitedly, 'reckon we'd have time to visit the *Queen Mary* while we're here?'

'But you've seen it once,' his mother remarked.

'Yeh, but I want to see it again. And I want to go over that weirdo's plane — you know, what's it called?'

'You mean Howard Hughes's *Spruce Goose*,' Chuck said, reaching across and tweaking his brother's ear.

Paul pushed Chuck's hand away. 'Yeh, that's it. Could we, Mom?'

'I don't see why not,' Marcia said, darting a look across the front seat at my uncle.

'Everything's okay by me,' my uncle said. 'I believe there's a special Fun Bus which shuttles people across to it. It operates out of the Disneyland Hotel. Should be easy.'

'I couldn't help feeling a surge of excitement about the whole planned trip.

'Gosh, isn't this fantastic?' I said, leaning forward as a large sign loomed up by the side of the road announcing Disneyland was straight ahead.

Chuck glanced at me and grinned. 'If you're a good little girl,' he said, 'I'll buy you a great big milkshake full of strawberry ice-cream, okay?'

If he thought he was going to dampen my happiness he was in for a shock. 'Hey,' I replied, smiling back at him, 'will it have a cherry on the top? I love cherries.'

Chuck sighed, and went back to stare out of the window, but not before I'd glimpsed a smile tugging at his lips, brightening his eyes.

Uncle Richard booked us in at the Disneyland Hotel and we decided to have our first visit to Disneyland that night.

'I've bought Unlimited Passports,' he explained. 'They give us our admission to the park plus all rides and attractions – it's much the easier way of organizing ourselves.' He handed out a small book of tickets to each of us.

Marcia placed an arm round my waist as we walked through the hotel's vast lobby. 'Some things have to be paid for separately,' she said, 'but your uncle and I insist this is our treat. So apart from any souvenirs you want to buy, Carol honey, plus of course things for that project you're going to do, everything else is on us, okay?'

I didn't know what to say. They were so kind and thoughtful. So I just nodded and smiled. 'Thank you, Aunt Marcia,' I said.

She gave me a hug. 'That was nice,' she said. I must have looked puzzled because she went on, 'You just called me *Aunt* Marcia for the first time. I kind of appreciate that.'

I hadn't realized it – that I hadn't called her aunt before, I mean; but now that I had, I intended to keep on because I could see it was important to her. It dawned on me then that maybe Marcia had been worried about meeting me, my liking her, just as I'd been worried about her. Strange, that had never occurred to me before.

Walking through the replica of an early nineteenth-century train station into Disneyland was like walking into wonderland! I'd read up about this incredible place – but seeing it was something else.

'Pretty, isn't it?' Marcia said, watching my expression. 'Walt Disney intended it to be the happiest place on earth – I think he just about made it.'

I just stood there, mesmerized. Everything was so beautiful. From the floodlit, majestic Matterhorn towering into the pitchy starlit Los Angeles night, to the speeding monorail. To one side I saw what I guessed were the ethereal spires of Sleeping Beauty's enchanted castle – looking so real I felt sure it must be at least three hundred years old.

'Well, where do we start?' my uncle asked. 'That's surely the question.'

'Let's go on the submerging submarine this time, Mom,' Paul pleaded.

'I want to make my way over to the Bear Country,' Chuck put in.

'Hold on there,' Uncle Richard said, 'or we'll all get lost. My plan is we take a trip on the old steam train to show Carol a general view of the whole area. Then later we'll take in one or two of the special attractions before having something to eat.'

'But, Mom. . .' Paul started, then stopped as we heard a series of explosions.

Marcia laughed, and slipped an arm through mine. 'Don't worry,' she said, 'that's the beginning of the parade down Main Street. Come on, if we hurry we'll catch it from the train.'

A few minutes later, I leaned out of the carriage window, craning my neck to catch as much of the carnival procession as I could. It was unbelievable. All the characters from Walt Disney's films were either on floodlit floats or else dancing along in the procession. As the whole parade wound its way along the mock nineteenth-century street, people clapped and generally joined in the merriment. It was like fairyland!

The train chugged its way past Main Street and we were carried on through the various sets – all spotlit and glittering, looking larger than life and yet at the same time incredibly real.

Chuck was busy taking photos when the train stopped at the station. I thought maybe I'd ask him if he'd let me have some prints when they were developed for my project, and for a second, that other photo came back into my mind – the one he'd taken of me – but I decided to forget about it for the time being. I didn't want anything to spoil this moment.

As we travelled through the night on the chuffing and puffing steam train, Uncle Richard and the others took great delight in pointing out the landmarks – Tomorrowland . . . Adventureland . . . Frontierland which, Paul explained excitedly, featured the roaring days of the Old West.

'Over there, see,' Chuck said, directing my attention through the window on the far side of the train, 'that's New Orleans Square. You should take a trip there. It shows how the city was way back in the 1850s. You know, when women wore long dresses and carried parasols . . . knew their places?'

If he was trying to rile me, he lost out. 'Oh,' I said feigning surprise, 'you mean when men were real gentlemen and didn't take advantage of their ladies?'

Uncle Richard laughed. 'I'd give up, Chuck if I were you,' he said, 'You've met your match with this young lady.'

Half an hour later, we stood by a brightly painted ice-cream parlour on one of the sidewalks, and made plans.

'Right, gang,' my uncle said, looking at his watch, 'we all meet back here in an hour. Okay?'

'Okay!' we replied.

'You going to be all right with Chuck?' Marcia asked. 'You can always come to It's A Small World with us if you'd rather.'

'Oh, come on, Mom,' Chuck said, grinning. 'If she thinks she's a toughie, let her come with me to the Bear Country jamboree. Then I'll take her over to the Haunted Mansion – that should help her sleep tonight.'

'Chuck,' Marcia began, throwing her son a warning glance.

'Don't worry, Aunt Marcia,' I said, 'I can take care of myself. He doesn't scare me!'

Everyone laughed.

'Fine — well don't forget we meet here at nine-thirty, by which time I should think we'll all be starving.' Uncle Richard gave me a special smile. 'You sure you'll be okay with Superman?' he asked.

'Sure,' I replied, shaking my head. 'Didn't you know I'm the original Spiderwoman?'

We parted company and Chuck beckoned me to follow him, then started at a quick pace picking his way through the crowds. I had to half-run to keep up with him, but there was no way I was going to ask him to slow down, was there? Spiderwoman wasn't that type!

It was an experience all too much for me! By the time Chuck and I staggered back to the prearranged meeting place my head was swimming from all the sights, bright lights and constant noise. I'd kept catching tantalizing, exciting glimpses of this set and that, and wanted to explore them all.

Bear Country had been fantastic, a real back-to-nature affair, and I could see that for all the bantering Chuck was really a keen naturalist.

The Haunted House was some experience, too! Especially the way they had ghostly figures dancing in the main hall of the house . . . you could actually see them dancing through the colonnades!

'How do they do that?' I'd asked.

'Holographs,' Chuck said, as if that explained everything.

'Oh, of course,' I'd replied, and I determined to look up what it was as soon as the opportunity occurred.

He'd seen my bewilderment though and added, 'It's all done with laser beams.'

Now, as we stood by the ice-cream parlour waiting for the others, I glanced up at him. He was busy watching the monorail circle overhead, unaware of the fact that I was studying him. He'd been great taking me around. Now I thought, if he weren't so sure of himself, so conceited, he'd be almost human.

'Look,' he said, turning his attention back to me. 'Let's go and wait in the ice-cream parlour. If we sit at one of the tables outside, the others will see us.'

'Okay,' I said, thankful for the idea of sitting down.

I followed his broad back up the steps and let him usher me to an empty table outside the café.

Pink-and-white candy-striped umbrellas shaded the tables, and the pink and white were picked up by the canvas chair. White paintwork and masses of potted plants gave the place a festival air.

It's rather like sitting in the centre of a stick of candyfloss, I thought.

'What would you like to drink while we wait?' Chuck asked, looking up from an elaborately printed menu, complete with pink tassel!

I shrugged, then said, 'Do I qualify for that milk-shake now?'

He smiled across at me. 'You mean the one with the cherry on top?' He'd remembered my words.

'The very same,' I said.

He studied my face for a long moment, a slightly puzzled expression in his eyes. 'You're a strange mixture,' he finally pronounced, then leaned over and tugged a strand of my hair.

I pulled away. 'Stop molesting me!' I told him, playfully. Then added, 'I bet you wouldn't do that to Danielle.'

Chuck scowled. 'If Danielle had a sense of humour she might see the funny side of me pulling her hair. But apart from her stunning good looks, there's very little else on offer.'

'I thought you and she "went back a long way"?' I said, using Marcia's expression.

Chuck looked round for the waiter, then beckoned the white-suited boy over. Before the waiter arrived, Chuck said, 'Sure we dated once.' He was watching to see my reaction, but I didn't move. The waiter arrived and having taken our order, left with a 'Thank you kindly, sir!'

Chuck put his head to one side, eyeing me with curiosity. 'I bet you dated when you were younger.'

I lowered my eyes remembering Martin Wilde and the brief episode with the flashing dark-eyed Ramon.

'I thought so,' Chuck said. 'Well, Danielle and I dated – but we were kids. It didn't mean anything to me. Maybe to her, but I doubt it. I found out she was dating other guys, too, so we broke up. Anyway, she'd never had a guy dump her. That's why she keeps trying to make a comeback. But it won't work with me. Satisfied?'

I chewed on my bottom lip, not knowing what to say.

The waiter returned carrying our order. He placed an enormous pink frothy milkshake in front of me, then a similar chocolate-coloured one before Chuck.

'Hey!' I said, pulling a face. 'No cherry!'

Chuck laughed and started sipping his drink through a bright green bendy straw. 'You don't need one,' he said between mouthfuls.

'But you promised,' I said, pretending to be upset.

'I'll get you one next time,' he was grinning at me.

'What next time?' I asked, suddenly coldly aware that although this was the first time I'd been to Disneyland, it was probably going to be the last time too. It was a depressing thought.

Chuck stopped drinking, leaned across and took my hand.

'Hey, cheer up,' he told me. 'Of course there'll be other times. You don't think we're going to lose contact once you go back to Wimbledon, do you?'

I gazed at him over the top of my milkshake. A pair of clear blue eyes looked back and then a peculiar thought materialized.

I'm in love with you, Chuck Walker, I thought.

'You look as though you want to tell me something,' Chuck said, eyeing me with a special new interest.

Oh no! I thought, he's reading my thoughts. I lowered my eyes and pretended to concentrate on my milkshake. I was trembling and my heart was pounding away as loud as the big bass drum that Goofy had been beating in the parade down Main Street.

'Do you want another drink?'

I wondered what Chuck was talking about and glanced down at my glass. I'd been so lost in my own thoughts that I'd finished my milkshake without realizing it.

I shook my head, not daring to speak in case my voice gave out. He kept holding my gaze till my cheeks grew hot. With great difficulty I tore my eyes away from his and looked out on to the sidewalk. Paul, Marcia and my Uncle were walking towards us. I'd never been so pleased to see anyone in my life!

'Hi! We're over here!' I shouted loudly. 'Hey!'

'There's no need to scream,' Chuck said, amused. 'They've heard you. Anyone would think you were scared to be alone with me.'

I turned on him, embarrassment and shyness making me nervous. 'Don't be stupid!' I said brightly, too brightly, my head spinning. 'Why should I be?'

He didn't answer. He didn't need to. His expression and the slight curl at the corner of his lips told me why. But it wasn't patronizing or conceited and I suddenly thought, crazily, *Does he love me, too*?

We were still gazing at each other when the others joined us.

'Right, let's go and get something to eat at one of the restaurants,' Marcia suggested. 'I just bet you're starving, aren't you, Carol sweet?'

I stared at her, starry eyed. I had been hungry, but now, for some odd reason, I wasn't. Not in the least.

The following five days in Los Angeles were a round of excitement, thrills and fun. And a growing, blossoming awareness that what I felt for Chuck wasn't a bit like the feelings I'd had for Martin, or Ramon. One moment I'd be flying high, feeling deliriously happy such as the time we stood in the centre of the round cinema in Tomorrow's World. The incredible sensation of watching a larger-than-life screening of a journey through America was nothing compared to the thrill of Chuck's fingers gently touching mine.

But then the happiness would disappear and the next moment I'd find myself wondering how I was ever going to be able to say goodbye to Chuck when the time came for me to fly back to England.

I was in a blue mood when we went to visit the famous Knotts Berry Farm. Chuck and I were watching the Calico Barn Dance when he slipped an arm along my shoulders.

'Don't do that!' I said, pulling away and glancing round, terrified in case the others had seen.

'Don't fret yourself, everyone's gone over to the Fiesta Village,' Chuck said. 'Relax.'

Relax? That was a joke! Couldn't he see that he made me nervous? I looked up at him to tell him to go away but at that moment he lowered his head and touched his lips to mine.

'I love you, Carol,' he whispered, a moment later.

'No, you don't!' I said curtly.

The softness flickered and died in his eyes. 'There you go again, Miss Knowall. Okay, so I don't love you,' he said, then grinned.

Confused, angry and hurt, I stood my ground. Me and my mouth! Why did I have to go and say that? Now I didn't know if he loved me or not.

'Oh, men!' I glared up at him – he grinned back. 'Stop laughing at me!' I said, my face burning.

'Stop acting like a child,' he retorted, still amused.

'I'm sixteen,' I said defiantly.

'You'll grow out of it, don't worry,' he responded.

'Chuck Walker I . . . I . . .' I was so furious I couldn't think of anything to say to get at him.

'You what?' he prompted, taking a step closer so that I actually had to raise my chin to stare up at him. And that's when it slipped out.

'I . . . I . . . I love you,' I whispered.

He smiled and nodded. 'Good. Well, now we've got that out of the way, let's go and enjoy ourselves.' He kissed me lightly again, then holding my hand he led me away from the dance, out into the searing sunlight.

The air smelt fresh and heady and a cool playful breeze lifted my hair away from my hot cheeks. I felt light-headed, dizzy, and as I followed Chuck towards the Fiesta Village, to join the others, I could have sworn I was walking on air!

Chapter 14

It was Saturday and we'd been back from LA a week. A week crammed with exciting days – golden days spent in the sun and sea. I'd met a whole bunch of Chuck's friends and between them I'd finally been taught how to surf-board. I wasn't as good as Danielle, that's for sure, but at least I'd stayed above the water – not under it!

Everyone seemed so friendly and relaxed. Chuck and I were included in picnics and parties and, one evening, ten of us piled into a collection of old cars and went to a drive-in movie. It was fantastic!

Later, someone suggested a beach party for the following Sunday.

'Is it okay if we go, Mom?' Chuck asked, now standing in the kitchen, popping corn in a large pan.

I sat on one of the high stools, leaning my chin on my hands watching him. The occasional *pop*! and *crack*! made me smile.

'What happens if you take the lid off?' I asked.

'Popcorn wallpaper!' Chuck grinned across at me. His smile made me feel warm and melty inside.

'Who's going, Chuck?' Marcia asked. She was standing opposite her son, mixing the syrup for the popcorn.

Chuck shrugged. 'Usual crowd, I guess.'

'I'm coming, too,' Paul said. 'Don't say I can't.'

'You can't!' Chuck threw in his brother's direction.

'Aw, Mom. . .' came the response, but Marcia

wasn't really listening. She was too concerned with finding a place to put the pan down on the working surface.

I shot off the stool and cleared a spot among the collection of boxes and packets.

'Thanks, hon,' she said, stirring the bubbling, browning mixture. The caramel smell made my mouth water. I loved watching the family pop the corn and had already bought the ingredients to take back to England with me, so that we could make some at home.

'What do you wear to a beach party?' I asked.

Paul snickered. 'Nothing,' he said.

'That's enough of that!' Marcia told him crossly.

'Well, it's true,' Paul said, pulling a face.

'It is not!' she said. 'Just because last year a couple of girls had too much to drink and got silly doesn't mean it's usual.'

I stared from one to the other and then over at Chuck. What sort of party was I letting myself in for?

Chuck gave the pan a last firm shake, then took it off the electric burner.

'Don't look so worried, Carol,' he said, catching me staring at him. 'It's not going to be an orgy or anything fancy like that. It's just a group of kids cooking corn over a fire and having a few cokes. It's fun – you'll enjoy it, trust me.' He took the lid off the pan, then passed the popped corn over to his mother.

Marcia poured the molasses-based syrup over the corn, and shook the pan vigorously.

'Okay, gang,' she said, tipping the warm, sticky mixture into a large basin, 'come and get it!'

The fire was already burning when Chuck and I arrived at the beach party. A couple of the girls who I recognized were busy placing foil-covered jacket potatoes in the ashes.

'Take the stuff we've brought over to the table by the rocks,' Chuck said. 'I'll give the other boys a hand with the ice-box for the drinks.'

I walked over to the table — two planks of wood supported on a jutting rock — and smiled at the girls who were busy preparing the food.

'Where do I put these things?' I asked.

One of the girls, her hair caught in a pony tail, reached out and took the carrier bag I was holding.

'I'll take it,' she said, and smiled. 'Want to lend a hand?'

'Sure,' I replied. 'Just show me what to do.'

'You could help wrap the rest of these corns if you like,' she said. 'They go with the potatoes in the embers.'

'Okay.' I walked over to where the ears of corn were stacked at one end of the table.

'Are you sure you don't mind?' the girl asked, smiling.

'Mind? Of course not!' I replied. 'Compared to my usual Sundays in London, this is Heaven!'

'You've got to be kidding,' Miss pony-tail said. 'How could anything be boring in a great place like London. Heck, I'd rather be in London than spend a whole summer here on the beach. Now that's boring! Believe me, there's a limit to how much sunbathing you can take.'

Her companion nodded in agreement. 'It's true,' she said. 'After the first month you might be brown — but boy, after that it's just plain mind-blowing!'

I couldn't believe my ears. How could life ever be boring if you lived in California? Yet, thinking about it as I wrapped the corn, I realized that maybe they had a point. It was all a matter of what you were used to.

I seemed to have wrapped a mountain of corn in foil and was just starting on another when Chuck came back.

'Hi, how you getting on?' he asked, slipping an arm round my waist. I could feel his warm fingers on my bare skin between my halter top and shorts.

'I think you should take her away and have a dance,' the pony-tail suggested, nicely. 'Or she could be here all night.'

'Why did you think I came over?' Chuck said. He bent his head and kissed the soft skin behind my ear. It tickled. Playfully, I pushed him away.

'Don't tell me you don't like it?' he said.

'I don't like it,' I teased.

'Come and tell me how much you don't like it while we're dancing.'

An old Bee Gees number floated over the beach

from a transistor rigged up in the back of a van. Chuck took me into his arms and we began to move slowly to the melody. I was aware of the salty smell of the sea, and the sand under my feet; of the crackling fire and star-filled sky. But most of all, I was aware of being held in Chuck's arms. We danced for a while and then Chuck suggested we got some refreshment.

'I'm having a can of beer,' he told me as we stood by some upturned crates set up as an improvised bar. 'What about you?'

For a moment I hesitated, wondering if I should have a beer, too. But the truth is, I don't like it, so I asked for a coke.

'Anything in it?' Chuck asked.

'Is there ice?'

Chuck laughed. 'I meant something stronger – like vodka or gin?'

'I don't like alcohol,' I said, then for some reason I added, 'I'm sorry.'

One of the girls near us looked over her shoulder. 'Is your date under age, Chuck?' she asked, grinning in the bright silvery moonlight.

I pretended not to hear and waited while Chuck found a can of coke, pulled the tab, and handed it to me.

'Come on, let's go grab a couple of hamburgers and some corn,' he suggested. 'All this outdoor activity makes me hungry.'

Thankfully, I followed him. But I couldn't help thinking maybe he was wishing he was with someone else. Someone as sophisticated as Danielle perhaps. Or some of the other girls who were drinking wine and apparently enjoying it.

As the evening wore on, it became obvious that some of the couples were wandering away from the general group, to the far end of the beach – to the privacy of the shadowed rocks. Did Chuck expect to do the same? I wondered. I tried to relax in his arms, but every time I saw another boy and girl, arms tightly round each other, break away from the dance area, I grew tense.

'Enjoying your first beach party?' Chuck asked, holding me close as we moved in time to Elvis's 'Love Me Tender'.

'Don't I act as if I am?' I pulled away and smiled up at him – he was giving me a quizzical look. 'What's wrong?' I asked.

'I was about to ask you the same. You seem so . . . well, nervous. What is it?'

I tried to laugh away his concern. 'Nervous? Of course I'm not,' I said, trying to sound convincing and failing. Then, changing the subject, I suggested we rested and had a drink.

'Whatever you say, ma'am,' he joked. He pulled me to him and, with his arm holding my waist tightly, led me off the dance area.

We helped ourselves to more drinks and stood watching the others dancing. The smoke from the fire spiralled up into the star-studded sky, the flames now only a luminous glow.

Someone behind us laughed and a girl giggled

hysterically. I looked over my shoulder. A group was huddled round the boot of a van in a semi-circle — passing a cigarette from mouth to mouth.

'Hey, dreamer, come back to me,' Chuck whispered in my ear and I felt his lips on my neck.

I pulled away, feeling uncertain. Out of my depth.

'Did I do something wrong?' Chuck asked, a hurt note in his voice.

'No – it . . . er . . . tickled, that's all,' I lied, glancing nervously across at him by the light of the moon.

For a long moment he didn't say anything. Then he shrugged, took my empty coke can and indicated the dance floor. 'Let's go dance,' he said, flatly.

A lump came to my throat. Why was I acting so dumb? What was I scared of? Heck! I thought, following Chuck on to the dance area, why can't I just relax and enjoy myself like all the others? But it was no good, I couldn't because all the time I kept thinking that at any moment Chuck would suggest we went for a walk along the deserted beach, and then what? It wasn't that I didn't trust Chuck, because I did. But did I trust me? It was all so romantic . . . the beach, the music and the moonlight. It was romantic all right, but something deep within me said no, it was all wrong.

The more we danced, the more confused I became. Half of me wanted to drift away with Chuck while the saner half of me kept pulling me back. And then something happened to stop my private emotional struggle.

Danielle arrived!

She came running and laughing down the beach with a bunch of other kids — mostly boys.

'Hey,' she called, spinning round, 'where's all the action? This party's more like an undertakers' night out!'

She turned and staggered a bit and I realized she'd been drinking. Her eyes rested on Chuck — and me. 'Well, look ye here, if it isn't little Miss London — the girl who likes swimming in fish ponds!' She laughed and made her way to stand by Chuck. 'How about all of us having a little fun?' she suggested, her words slightly slurred. 'How about you,' she tapped a long nail on Chuck's broad chest, 'and me swimming out to the platform? I've some champagne for the winner.'

'Another time,' Chuck said, pleasantly. 'I'm afraid I haven't any trunks with me.'

Danielle laughed suggestively. 'Me neither,' she giggled. Then added, 'But that's not going to put me off. Anyway,' she glanced around at a group of boys who had come down to the beach with her, 'if you're chicken there are plenty of others here who aren't so shy. But then you weren't either, in the past, were you, Chuck?'

I felt the blood racing to my cheeks. 'I think I'll go and get another coke,' I said, backing away from the scene.

Danielle turned on me and smiled viciously. 'Do that, sugar pie,' she said, her large eyes glinting dangerously, 'after all, you do seem to be cramping lover-boy's style. He doesn't usually run around with kids.'

I glanced at Chuck, humiliated, and yet feeling powerless to do anything about it ... wanting him to spring to my defence. But he just stood there, staring at the smiling girl who was facing him.

'Okay, boys,' Danielle said, 'who's going to compete with Chuck and me for the champagne?' Then she turned back to Chuck who seemed frozen where he stood. 'Ready?' she cooed and began to shrug off the shoestring straps of her sundress.

The dress drifted over her tanned shoulders and slid gracefully around her feet. I just caught sight of her gleaming bare body before I turned and stumbled blindly up the beach.

I hadn't even reached the Honda before a pair of strong hands grabbed me and spun me round.

'Carol, wait! I'm sorry,' Chuck said, breathlessly.

I stared wide-eyed at him. 'Leave me alone!' I shouted. 'Go away!'

'Carol I —' Chuck began, but I cut him off.

'Why did you bring me here?' I demanded. 'Why? You knew how it would be. Did you think I'd be like all the others? Swayed by the music and the moonlight? Did you think I'd be happy to do what most of the others are doing? Well, you were wrong, weren't you?' Tears of self-pity and anger engulfed me. But I couldn't stop them. 'Don't you worry about me,' I spat at him. 'I may be a kid, as Danielle said, but I can look after myself.' I turned and began to walk away from the parking lot. I didn't even stop to think where I was going.

'Carol, don't be such a baby!' Chuck called, running up and taking my arm.

I pulled away, furiously. 'That's just it, isn't it?' I shouted, tears running freely down my face. 'To you I am a baby. Well, let me tell you something — I'm glad. I like being a baby and, just for the record, I'll grow up when *I* want to, not just to follow the crowd. So go on — go and join your sophisticated, grown-up Danielle.'

Chuck didn't make a move.

'Well,' I cried, sniffing back fresh tears, 'why don't you go?'

'Because I want to be with you,' he said, quietly.

We stood staring at each other for a moment, then I said, 'You do?'

He nodded.

'Come on, Carol,' he said, gently taking my hand in his. 'Let's go home.'

Chuck stopped the car under one of the redwood trees at the side of the house, then switched off the engine.

I sat very still, staring through the windscreen, thinking. Then slowly I turned to face Chuck and, reaching up, kissed him on his cheek.

'What's that all about?' He sounded puzzled.

I shrugged. 'Because I think I love you,' I said.

'Only think?'

I nodded, then closed my eyes. I didn't want to say anything to hurt him but at the same time I wanted to try to explain how I felt.

'Chuck,' I said, smiling at him, 'I know this may sound crazy, but maybe Danielle was right. Maybe you were. Maybe I am still too young.' He tried to interrupt me but I placed a finger on his warm lips. 'I've had time to think on the journey back here. Down on the beach I was all confused. I felt, well, pressured. Then Danielle arrived – and in a way she did me a favour.'

'How's that?' Chuck asked, not sounding at all convinced.

I looked across at him, trying to make out the contours of his face in the darkness.

'She gave me time to breathe,' I said. 'Chuck, I do like being with you. And I like touching you and kissing you – but I don't know if that's love. I don't even think I know what love is – yet.'

'Yet?'

I laughed softly. 'Do you?' I asked.

He didn't answer at first, then he sighed. 'I guess not,' he agreed. Then qualified it by saying, teasingly, 'Yet.'

'Then you're not angry – or hurt?'

'I should be,' he said, but there was a lightness in his voice. 'After all, most girls have the habit of falling madly in love with me on first sight.'

I laughed. 'My first glimpse of you found me in a very uncomfortable position,' I reminded him. 'And I won't go back to England until I have that negative, either.'

'We'll see,' he teased.

I went to open the car door but Chuck stopped me.

'Let me know if you come to any decision about me, won't you?' he asked.

I nodded. 'But first I've got a lot of things to sort out.'

'About me?' Chuck asked, trying to see my expression.

'No,' I told him. 'Not about you – about me.'

Chuck leaned across and lifted the door handle. Then he looked up and planted a light kiss on my cheek. 'You know something,' he said, softly, and when I didn't answer he continued, 'you're very special.'

'Like a cherry on a milkshake?' I asked, swinging my legs out of the car.

'Better!' he called after me as I started for the house.

Chapter 15

'Okay, troops,' Uncle Richard said as we all piled into the Dodge, 'where to now?'

Chuck, Paul and I had just walked up Lombard Street – the most crooked street in the world – to meet Marcia and my uncle in the car at the top.

We had been sightseeing in San Francisco all day, arriving soon after nine; now it was nearly seven

My head still buzzed with all the beautiful places I'd seen and all the things I'd done.

Chuck had kept his promise and we'd taken a cable car ride over the seven hills. I felt just like Judy Garland in her old movie as we were shaken and jogged, and the bell kept ringing as people wanted to get off, while others crowded on.

Then we'd visited Fisherman's Wharf and joined the tourists on a boat trip round the notorious fortress of Alcatraz, while seagulls swooped and dived overhead, catching food thrown to them by the passengers.

We'd had a snack lunch of hot clam chowder on the wharf and some crab claws, all washed down with chilled fresh orange juice.

Most of the afternoon we'd spent exploring the Golden Gate Park and wandering round the magnificent Oriental Tea Gardens with their granite shrine and delicate arched bridge which, Uncle Richard had pointed out, was built in the shape of a drum. Chuck took me to visit the De Young Museum, and later we joined the others, on the smooth lawns, as they rested under a vast pine tree.

It had been a day to remember, and my shoulder bag was bursting with all the postcards and booklets I'd collected for my project which I planned to write up the moment I returned to England.

'I vote we head for Chinatown,' Marcia said. 'I know it's early, but I'm dying to have dinner. How about you?'

'Great!' Paul Junior agreed, jumping up and down. 'Come on then, let's go!'

'How about you two?' Uncle Richard asked. 'Do you think an authentic Chinese meal will go down well?'

'You bet!' Chuck said, settling his great shoulder against my arm in the back seat.

I nodded enthusiastically. I'd heard so much about the restaurants and charm of Chinatown that I was dying to see it.

An hour later we'd parked the car and were wandering along Grant Avenue, which, Chuck had explained, was the main thoroughfare in the Chinese quarter of the city. Everywhere I looked I saw cast-iron grilled balconies and delicate pagoda towers; Oriental lanterns, softly glowing; and gaily lighted shop windows. It was a never-to-be-forgotten experience ... but then I thought, sadly, it had been a never-to-be-forgotten holiday.

As if sensing my sadness, Chuck slipped an arm along my shoulders.

'What are you thinking?' he asked.

I sighed. 'About this street, about the city. About this last four weeks,' I said. 'I can't believe it's nearly over.'

'There's always next year,' he said, trying to cheer me up.

I smiled up at him. 'Yes, there is,' I said. 'Or the next one, I guess.' We walked along in silence listening to the patter of Chinese as people passed us. Each of us were lost in our own thoughts.

'Will you write?' he asked, at last.

'Of course,' I said. 'If you do.'

'It's a promise then?' he said, stopping under a street lamp.

'It's a promise,' I agreed. I think he would have kissed me there and then if Uncle Richard hadn't called to us from a brightly lit restaurant doorway.

We smiled at each other and then ran, hand in hand, to join the others.

Chapter 16

'Hey, Carol!'

I looked up from writing my homework timetable in my exercise book. 'What?' I asked.

Claire scrambled across the desks and came to sit by me. We were the last ones in the classroom and I was anxious to finish and get home.

'What are you planning to do this weekend?' she asked. 'If you're not doing anything special I thought maybe you'd like to come to the cinema with me.'

I finished my notes, then closed my book and dropped it into my holdall. 'I'm sorry,' I said 'but I've got so much to do, I can't.'

Claire looked disappointed. 'You trying to play hard to get or something?' she asked, miserably.

'Don't be daft!'

'Yes? Well this is the third weekend since you've come back from your trip that you've been busy.'

'Well, I'm sorry,' I said, seeing the disappointment on her face. 'But it's the truth.'

'What are you doing then?' she demanded.

'Well, I've got my project to finish off and then Mr Prentis suggested I write an essay on my holiday for the school magazine. And that's got to be in by this coming Wednesday. And I want to get to the library and get some books on America —'

'What for?' Claire asked, surprised.

I shrugged. 'Because I'm interested in finding out more about it. You never know when I might get another chance to go back.'

Claire mulled this over for a while. 'Is that going to take your whole weekend up?' she said.

I was going to tell her that I also had another job to do — except that it wasn't a job at all. It was a pleasure. My weekly letter to Chuck.

Chuck . . . I thought about him with his easy smile and quick humour.

'I want that photo of me before I go,' I'd demanded the last night — and he'd laughed.

'I never did take it,' he told me.

'You did!' I said. 'I saw your finger move on the shutter.'

'Believe me, Carol — I was pretending. It's the truth,' he said. Then grinned. 'I guess I'm too young for that sort of photograph,' he'd said.

We'd both laughed then, and he'd taken me in his

arms and gently kissed me. I could still feel the warmth of his lips, even now. . .

'Carol, are you still with me?'

I snapped back to the present. Claire was looking at me questioningly. 'Are you okay?' she asked.

I laughed and jumped up. 'I'm fine,' I said.

Then gathering my jacket and bag together we started walking to the door.

'Look,' I said as we reached the cloakroom, 'I've got an idea. Why not pop over on Sunday afternoon and I'll make us some popcorn?'

'Popcorn!' Claire exclaimed.

'Yes, popcorn,' I said, laughing at her surprise. Then as she continued to stare at me as if I were mad, I added, 'It's an old-fashioned American custom. You'll love it!'

It was raining on Sunday and outside on the Common great puddles were appearing. The sky was grey and there was definitely a feeling of autumn in the air.

But in our kitchen, there was a delicious smell of hot molasses and the sound of popping corn as I shook the pan over the gas flames.

Claire watched me from the kitchen table, where she sat chewing on a nail.

'What are you looking at?' I asked, grinning.

'You,' she replied.

I raised my eyebrows at her. 'Oh, why?'

She shrugged and, taking her hands away from her mouth, sat on them. She sat studying me, swaying on her seat.

'I don't know, you seem ... well, different somehow,' she said.

'I feel different,' I told her, happily. And I did. And then I suddenly thought, well, I guess growing up's not so bad after all.

I thought back to the beginning of the year, to before my trip ... before Chuck, and it seemed a million years ago. I smiled to myself as I remembered how worried I'd been about even going – of taking that first tentative step towards the day when I'd begin making a life for myself. Now I realized there was nothing to be frightened about. The secret was to take a step at a time. Just one at a time. That's all.

Anita Eires
Spanish Exchange 85p

Margarita had only been in Madrid a few hours when she knew just how exciting her Spanish holiday was going to be. Her handsome cousin Roberto had changed a lot since his trip to England two summers before. Then, in Marbella, she met Rafael with his motorboat, his startling blond hair and his gorgeous tan. Everything was going to be wonderful except for one thing about Rafael that Margarita had yet to learn.

Tug of Love 85p

Since her mother's death her father had meant everything to sixteen-year-old Maria. To hurt him would be worse than hurting herself. But Joey had drifted into her life that summer and Maria wanted to follow him whatever the cost. From the moment she heard his first hello she had known that choice didn't come into it – when you're in love you only listen to your heart.

Summer Awakening 85p

It was to be the holiday of a lifetime – two weeks in a villa in sunny Majorca. The whole family expected fun, sun and adventure, but when Lainie packed her daring new pink bikini she didn't expect the excitement of a boy as handsome and wealthy as Jonty. Could a holiday romance last? Lainie wasn't going to think about it – why worry about tomorrow when there is love in the sun and the sea?

Pam Lyons
A Boy Called Simon 85p

When Gabrielle's father's business crashed it changed the lives of the whole family. Their beautiful house in the country had to be sold; Gabby had to leave the boarding school and all her friends. Her parents' marriage was crumbling and life in the city suburbs promised nothing but sorrow and heartache. Then, on a never-to-be-forgotten night, a boy called Simon walked into her life.

It Could Never Be 85p

Ever since her father left home Cathy's world had been just her and her mum and her dog, Heinz. Then one night her glamorous mother brought a man home for dinner. He was charming, good-looking and twenty-five. Cathy thought he was much too young for Mum; that it was really herself that he was interested in. Those roses *must* have been for her.

He Was Bad 85p

For Hazel there was nothing quaint or cute about being an identical twin. She was eleven when she struck her first blow for freedom, and from then on it was a no holds barred effort to untwin herself. Then she met Rolo. No parents would approve of a boyfriend who was a biker and the leader of a gang. But why should Hazel care what they thought? They didn't care for her. It was only later that the heartache began.

Mary Hooper
Follow that Dream 85p

Her parents' dream of moving to Cornwall is a nightmare blow for
Sally. How could she bear to leave London and be stuck away in the
country . . . with no mates, no music, no decent clothes, no parties
and no Ben, just when she was getting somewhere with him? But
the long-awaited visit from her best friend, Joanne, brings some
unexpected conflicts and Sally finds her determination to remain
apart slowly undermined by the presence of a boy called Danny . . .

Love, Emma 85p

Emma begins her training with high hopes. Determined to achieve
something for herself, she still finds the three-year separation from
her established world of family and friends a little frightening. In
letters to her parents, best friend and boyfriend – and in entries in
her secret diary – Emma describes her new world in warm and witty
detail . . . hard-working, occasionally exciting and always exhausting –
but there are rewards; *and* a student doctor named Luke . . .